OUT OF THIS WORLD

Ali Sparkes

OXFORD
UNIVERSITY PRESS

OXFORD
UNIVERSITY PRESS

Great Clarendon Street, Oxford OX2 6DP

Oxford University Press is a department of the University of Oxford.
It furthers the University's objective of excellence in research, scholarship,
and education by publishing worldwide in

Oxford New York

Auckland Cape Town Dar es Salaam Hong Kong Karachi
Kuala Lumpur Madrid Melbourne Mexico City Nairobi
New Delhi Shanghai Taipei Toronto

With offices in

Argentina Austria Brazil Chile Czech Republic France Greece
Guatemala Hungary Italy Japan Poland Portugal Singapore
South Korea Switzerland Thailand Turkey Ukraine Vietnam

Oxford is a registered trade mark of Oxford University Press
in the UK and in certain other countries

British Library Cataloguing in Publication Data

Data available

ISBN: 978-0-19-279412-3

1 3 5 7 9 10 8 6 4 2

Printed in Great Britain
Paper used in the production of this book is a natural,
recyclable product made from wood grown in sustainable forests.
The manufacturing process conforms to the environmental
regulations of the country of origin.

JF

Many thanks to Ben McNutt of Woodsmoke, for the bushlore detail and to countryside rangers like Peter Potts, who teach, protect, guide, and inspire (and yes Pete—that *is* your bungalow), and to Tania, wherever you may be, for the outlaw games on the edge of the woods.

And a big helloooo to Townhill
Junior School in Southampton.
(You know why!)

Chapter 1

What would it be like when his brain exploded?

Would it go with a dull thud and just collapse inside his skull, or with a crack, flying in all directions? The sensible part of Tyrone knew that, of course, his brain *wouldn't* explode. You never heard of boys' heads exploding at the dentist, did you? Or maybe they just covered it up. Or maybe he was about to be the first . . .

He wasn't even having a filling. He could handle *that*. He didn't really mind the injection, and, although it *did* sound like his mouth had been invaded by a crazed killer wasp, he could just about put up with the drilling bit as well.

Somehow, the quiet, the concentration in *this* visit was much, much worse.

'Nearly done,' said John, his dentist. A cheerful man who wore bright jumpers and was persistently nice to people, he always insisted on being called John. Not

Mr Payne. Well, come to think of it, Mr Payne wasn't a great name for a dentist.

Right now John was cheerfully trying to drag Ty's brain out through his mouth. At least that's what it felt like with every twist and tweak. And even when he was done, and Ty could go, the horror of all this wouldn't be over. John was attaching a brace to Ty's teeth. It would be there for at least six months, pulling, dragging, pinching and bullying his rowdy, untidy teeth into shape.

'Just try to relax now,' said John. 'Won't be much longer.' As he'd been making similar promises for the last forty-five minutes, Ty wasn't inclined to believe him. He badly wanted to say something sarcastic like, '*You* try relaxing when you've got a scrap metal yard, eight fingers and a sucky nozzle thing shoved in your mouth!' but obviously he couldn't. He gurgled in a sarcastic way, but John and his nurse didn't notice.

Ty sighed, tried to be positive—his mum promised he'd have teeth like a film star when it was all over—and listened to Radio 2, which was always playing gently in the background, presumably to soothe patients. Unfortunately, it was the news, and nothing soothing ever got said in the news. Several countries were on the brink either of war or famine. A pop star was having a baby. A submarine, containing nearly sixty unfortunate Royal

Navy sailors, had sunk to the bottom of the North Sea and no-one knew how to get them up.

'OK—all done now,' said John, and took everything—except the brace—out of Ty's mouth. Ty sat up and said 'Wirrohrr,' in a mad, raspy voice.

'Sorry, dear?' said the nurse, taking his hand in hers.

'Wirrohrr, cleash,' said Ty, dribbling pathetically. She squeezed his hand and then handed him a small mirror. It was a magnifying one. In it, Ty's mouth looked like the Sydney Harbour Bridge. He groaned, shook his head, and then, remembering his manners, said 'Shankoo werry wuch,' and trudged glumly out of the surgery.

'You'll get used to it soon—and you'll speak just fine by tomorrow,' John called after him, still horribly cheerful.

In his blazer pocket, a few coins rattled a reminder that he now had to catch the bus right back to school in time for afternoon lessons. Other kids' mums would've picked them up and taken them home for chicken soup or something, he was sure. But his mum was on a ship by now, being the singer in a band which entertained people on cross-channel ferries.

Still, he thought, clambering onto the Number 5 and trying to say 'Swiftwood School please' without opening his lips, if he was lucky the metal in his mouth *wouldn't* attract passing Russian space debris down out of its orbit and the bus would get there on time. Hang on though, what was *lucky* about that?

'Hey! Tyrone—glad you could join us!' Mr Brading, the English teacher, slouched back in his chair as Ty sidled into the classroom. 'Dentist was it?'

Ty nodded, willing his teacher to leave it at that and let him get to his desk without talking. But Mr Brading was the kind of teacher who believes he's very, very funny, and all the pupils love him when he jokes.

'New brace then, is it?' he thundered. A snicker ran around the room like an evil sprite, hopping from desk to desk of all Ty's meaner classmates.

Ty gave Mr Brading a tight smile and headed for his seat.

'Never mind, you'll be able to pick up Sky One now,' said Mr Brading, adding his guffaw to the snickering. Everyone had now joined in. Ty pretended to be amused, laughing politely through his nose as he sat down. A sharp jab in between his shoulder blades indicated that Dom McGill had thought up another use for his pencil (normally only employed to pick his nose).

'Never mind, Scrap Gob,' he hissed. 'You were ugly anyway.'

'OK class!' shouted Mr Brading, walking up and down like a film director and flicking back his floppy brown hair. 'A scene from *Romeo and Juliet*! Page 55 of *Shakespeare for All*. Who can help me out here? Rebecca, you I think and—and . . .'

No! thought Ty. He couldn't! He *wouldn't!*

He would.

'. . . Tyrone, I think, can be our Romeo.'

Rebecca began to read, and Tyrone flicked to page 55.

At her pause, he lifted his woeful face, pulled his sore lips back over what felt like a souvenir chunk of the Eiffel Tower and read: 'Buck lo! Thizth the Eashth and Wooliet isshh ve shun . . .' The class—and every last hope in his heart—collapsed.

Dom McGill wasn't the brightest boy in Swiftwood School, but he was probably the biggest. His hands were huge and invariably clenched. When Dom decided to hit you it was a lot like being struck with a frozen chicken.

Today, though, Dom was having more fun with his mouth. Being not the brightest boy in Swiftwood School, he was quite delighted that he'd found a good jeering name for Ty so quickly. He felt it would last for the rest of the day, so he wouldn't have to think of another one until tomorrow.

Dom and his mates hung around by the school gates, poised like a church choir on Christmas Eve. As soon as Ty made an appearance, head down, hauling his over-weight schoolbag across his shoulder, Dom raised his hand like a conductor, lifted his corned-beef chin and counted the gang in . . .

'Scrap Gob! Scrap Gob! Scrap Gob! Scrap Gob!' With only two notes to play with, the boys managed to get an amazing amount of feeling into their chant. They conveyed, with a sneering lilt, that Ty was not only a geek, stuck up, and ugly, but also that, if they had half a chance, they would cheerfully give him the kind of pasting which would smear him all over the toilet block.

Rod, who was *slightly* sharper than the rest, got into the whole chant thing so much that he even attempted a rhyme. 'Scrap Gob, Scrap Gob, get yourself a—big—job . . .' The others looked at him, confused. It messed up the rhythm a bit and didn't make sense. This distracted them while Ty ducked in among a crowd of girls and crept out past them.

By the time they'd rallied and got into the next round of Scrap Gobbing, Ty was halfway up the road.

'Oi! Scrap Gob's getting away!' yelled Dom, and the mob bundled out after him.

It was a hot July day, and Ty was sweating by the time he reached the cut across the wasteland behind his house. His pursuers were only seconds behind him, tearing up a narrow alley between the old back-to-back houses. He could hear them puffing for breath and Rod's squeaky voice still gamely shouting 'Scrap Gob! Get Scrap Gob!'

The wasteland was the length of a football pitch, but would have been useless for a game. Covered in mounds of old rubble, sheets of rusting corrugated iron and discarded rubbish, its grass grew as high as his waist, hiding ruts and potholes which could twist an ankle if you didn't know where you were treading.

Happily, Ty knew exactly where he was treading. This was *his* patch. He knew he couldn't make it across without being seen and followed all the way back home. The mob was too close on his heels. He darted to his right, skirting the high, brittle wall boundary which separated the ground from the small backyards of the old houses.

In three seconds he reached a culvert which drained rainwater off the site and into an underground stream. It was only a metre or so deep and should have been covered, but its access cover had been up-ended years ago and never replaced. Ty dropped silently into the quiet gloom of the culvert, which was completely dry in the heat of summer. The grass that grew thick around it waved high over his head. Unless you knew where to look, you'd have no clue it was there. He was hidden and still, like a lizard under a stone.

Dom, Rod and three other boys rounded the corner of the alley and spread out into the wasteland. 'He's gone!' gasped Dom, his voice thick with disappointment and unspent violence. Rod and another boy cantered ahead, still enthusiastic. In the shade of the culvert, Ty grinned and stifled a snort as he heard Rod stumble into one of the trusty potholes and give a shrill shriek. 'Ah— nah! I've broken my bleedin' ankle!'

The city council had been promising for years to tidy up the wasteland and make a proper turfed 'green space' of it one day. As he heard Dom's gang retreating, telling Rod to stop being such a girl and muttering promises to get Scrap Gob later, Ty hoped that day would never come.

Chapter 2

'Hiya, babe . . .' Ty felt a familiar droop at his Aunty Dawn's distracted greeting. As usual, she was in the kitchen, leaning on the side, watching *The Teddy Taylor Talk Show* on the little portable TV next to the microwave.

A bag of cheesy curls lay open by her right arm and her hand worked in and out of it like a mechanical digger, shovelling the orangey nuggets into her mouth every few seconds while her eyes never strayed from the small screen, where Teddy Taylor's minders were holding apart two heavily made-up women who seemed to want to pull each other's hair out. Teddy Taylor himself was standing off to the side, holding his microphone, his suit and dyed blond hair immaculate, wearing an expression of mild compassion and dismay.

In some ways, Aunty Dawn was like his mum. She had the same wide, well shaped mouth and dark brown eyes. But her nose was shorter, her dark hair fluffier and she was quite a bit heavier. Ty's mum worked hard to keep her figure. She had to; she was an entertainer. Aunty Dawn worked from home. Apparently. Ty had never seen her do a stroke of work. It was something to do with telesales, his mum said. But it was lucky for them that she was so flexible (Ty had a mental image of Aunty Dawn trying to touch her toes and falling into the cat litter tray) because it meant she could be around at their place when mum had a gig and couldn't be there. Ty's dad had died when he was just a baby.

So Aunty Dawn was his guardian roughly half of the week. Guardian was probably a bit strong, thought Ty, heading upstairs to dump his school bag and peer unhappily into the bathroom mirror at his horrific mouth. If Aunty Dawn was guardian of anything in his house it was the telly and the fridge.

'I AM DAWN!' Ty suddenly declared, flicking back an imaginary cloak and giving his reflection a steely gaze. 'GUARDIAN OF THE FRIDGE, PROTECTOR OF THE CHEESY CURLS! And this . . .' he walked across the landing and peered down the stairwell into the open plan kitchen at his aunt, lost in a TV debate about tattooing, '. . . is my domain!'

It wasn't that he disliked his aunt. She was cheerful enough company and she didn't tell him off. In a way that was the point. She didn't tell him off because she didn't really notice him. There was a good chance that she wouldn't look at him between now and next Christmas, so there would certainly be no discussion about his new brace. No sympathy, and certainly no special tea-time treat to make him feel better, which his mum would surely have offered if only he'd had his mouth done at the end of the week when she was here.

And she *would* be here at the other end of this week, Ty told himself firmly, even though experience had taught him that quite possibly, she wouldn't be.

Feeling sorry for himself, Ty changed out of his school clothes and into his jeans, T-shirt and trainers. By the time he'd cut himself some bread and cheese, while Aunty Dawn laughed and nodded at the TV, he was feeling better. Even the difficulty of getting his tea past his brace (he later had to gouge a fair bit of it out with the handle of a teaspoon) didn't dampen his mood too much—tonight he'd be up at Kestrel's Croft with Sam, catching moths.

Sam was a countryside ranger. Ty had met him a couple of times on school trips and then when he'd joined the Young Naturalists' Club had been pleased to find Sam was one of the people running it. Sam was brilliant. Different. He was probably in his late twenties, Ty guessed, and completely mad about insects. He loved all wildlife but insects were really his thing. He ran tours for schools and other groups, taking them deep into the woods around the city, showing them how to spot where wild creatures had been, pointing out the deadliest fungi, and holding out amazing tiny creatures in the palm of his hand for everyone to stare at.

'This,' he'd say, 'is a shield bug. Also known as a stink bug. If you ever scare it, you'll know why. It shoots out an evil stink which sticks to your skin for days if you're unlucky enough to get the full blast.'

'Here,' he'd say, 'Look—this is the easiest way to get yourself some emergency rope.' And he'd seize a great long stinging nettle in his bare hand. Then he'd hold the root and shoot his clenched fingers up the stalk, whipping off all the leaves.

'Doesn't that hurt?!' winced Ty.

'Nope. Not when you do it like this—and look . . .' he'd looped and twisted the stem and tugged hard on it. 'Emergency rope. You can build a shelter using this stuff.'

Sam and Ty got to be friends. Sam had even shown Ty his moth collection back at his ranger's bungalow on the edge of Kestrel's Croft. He had hundreds of them. Some dead, some alive, some comatose in margarine tubs in his fridge. You had to be careful how you went about making a sandwich at Sam's.

The bungalow had a bedroom and a kitchen, a bathroom and a sitting room, but there was hardly anywhere to sit. Every surface had something weird or wonderful on it, from ancient knotty branches that Sam was halfway through whittling, to boxes of birds' feathers, casts of deer tracks and beautiful, papery wasps' nests. It didn't smell like a house. It smelled like a wood. Like a den.

Sam's den was fifteen minutes' bike ride away from Ty's house. He made it there by early dusk. Ty knocked on the door and it swung open. 'Come and get one, Ty,' called Sam, handing him a large round box-like thing, made of light, silvery metal.

Sam, a well built man with close cropped fair hair and dark grey eyes, emerged with another round box and a backpack on, which was full, Ty knew, of ropes and sugar and wine.

There were two good ways of trapping moths. One was to use the light traps which they were carrying— big reflective boxes with bright lights inside, which lured in the moon-seeking insects and kept them safely trapped until morning. The other way was to get them drunk.

Sam and Ty crunched across the dry woodland floor in the dimming light, heading for trees on the edge of a clearing, which had some good, low-hanging boughs. Ty climbed into one of them, and hauled up the ropes Sam passed to him, looping them securely around the strong branches. Then Sam made up the glutinous mixture of red wine and sugar, which he passed up to Ty in a flask.

'It's pretty muggy. I hope the storm stays off the mainland until we've got our moths,' said Sam, as Ty dripped the wine carefully down the ropes until they were blood red and giving out a sweet, heady smell.

'How's your mouth feeling?' Sam asked. Ty realized this was the first sympathetic question he'd had about his new brace.

'A bit sore. And my teeth feel kind of tickly—like I want to scratch my gums or something,' he said. 'But at least I can speak OK now. When they first went in my lips were swollen.'

'Bad luck,' said Sam, with feeling. 'It'll be worth it in the end. Just keep your head down,' he added, knowingly. He was well aware of the trouble that Ty had with bullies at school. Sam knew what it was like to be laughed at for something you couldn't help.

The sky was darkening now. To the east, fingers of purple reached across and to the west, as the sun sank into the trees, fat, bubbling clouds piled up in great pink pillars. A flash lit them up for a microsecond.

'Ah rats!' cursed Sam. 'Looks like it might hit us after all, although the forecast did say it was staying off the mainland tonight.'

Three other volunteers had joined them. Within an hour, they had six rope traps set up and the warm evening was steeped in the scent of sweet red wine.

Sam and Ty set up the light traps at the foot of the trees. Some moths would just go for the lights but others—often the rarer species—would drift towards the ropes and drink the sugary wine. Their feet would stick and they would have to stay put, unharmed and intoxicated, until morning, when they could be identified and counted before being freed.

By 9 p.m. everything was set and the volunteers were departing. 'Better get home, Ty,' said Sam. 'I'll see you back to the road.' As they set off there were one or two flashes again in the night sky. 'Hang on!' said Sam. 'I just want to double-check the lids of the light traps. If it does rain they could get swamped. Wait here a minute, Ty.'

Ty stood while Sam disappeared into the darkening wood. The birds had stopped their pre-roost chatter and a few owls were calling. Suddenly, there was a brilliant flash, much brighter than any so far. To Ty, it seemed almost green.

'Whoa! Sam! Did you see that?!' he called out. He held his breath and waited for the thunder, which surely must follow. But after several seconds, it was still quiet. Odd, thought Ty. Then something caught his eye. Several yards away, beneath some holly trees, something was glinting.

Ty wandered across, thinking it might be a glow-worm. Although it was a little late in the year for glow-worms to be out. Probably just a bit of plastic, reflecting, he thought. But the glinting was surprisingly steady— almost a glow. Kneeling on a tussock of cool grass, Ty peered down into the crispy layer of brown holly leaves and peat. There it was.

About the size of a chestnut, bizarre and beauti-ful, lay a lump of . . . what? Metal? Crystal? Rock? It was hard to tell. It glowed gently and glimmered at the edges, sometimes green, sometimes purple, then blue and now—red! Fascinated, Ty picked it up. It was weighty, like metal. Between his fingers it felt both crys-talline, as if it were covered in tiny jagged shards, and yet smooth. The thing rolled, almost trickled down his curved fingers into his palm.

And there it seemed to *nestle*. When Ty closed his fingers over it and squeezed, he felt is if it was very slightly *giving*. And yet, when he opened them again and stared at the strange nugget, it was smooth and hard. The dancing, glimmering light that had caught his attention, now settled into a steady purple glow.

Ty sniffed it. He could only smell the earthy scent of his own skin. Carefully, he put his lips to it. It was warm but perfectly solid now. What on earth was it?

'Ty! Where are you?' Sam was back. Ty leaped up and went across to him.

'I've just found something really weird,' he said.

'Oh? What's that then?'

Ty opened his palm, but the thing was darker now, and with the failing light, could barely be seen. Perhaps it was just a pebble, after all.

'There's not enough light,' he said. 'I'll bring it after school tomorrow, if you're around.'

'Sure. I will be,' said Sam. 'Thanks for your help. You can come and see what we've found. Looks like the storm's going to miss us after all. OK—you all right to carry on from here?'

They had reached the main road that flanked the nature reserve. Ty had left his bike chained up at a lamp-post here.

'Yeah! Fine. See you tomorrow.'

As Sam vanished back into the wood, Ty slid the strange thing in his palm into his jeans pocket. He undid his bike chain with some difficulty, as the numbers on the combination lock kept spinning off in all directions—*and* the lamppost light suddenly fizzed and went out above him.

'Cheers!' said Ty, glaring at the dead bulb. 'Oh—brilliant!' Now his front headlight had gone dark, with a slight pop. The red one at the rear flashed three times before the ruby glare seeped away to nothing.

Ty cycled home in the dark, the strange metallic thing oddly warm in his pocket. He didn't notice several more street lights flare and then lapse into darkness as he passed.

Chapter 3

He'd been dribbling in his sleep. Ty was disgusted when he woke up and found his pillow soggy. Bleakly, he realized that his new brace was probably the reason for it and gloom crept up and rode piggyback on his disgust.

Down in the kitchen, Aunty Dawn was trying to eat a Pop Tart. Clad in her saggy violet dressing gown, she was going 'Ha-ah—ha-uh—ooh—hah!', chucking the perilously hot, sugar topped square from finger to finger. She still couldn't resist biting into it though, and promptly burned her mouth, resuming the 'Ha-ah—aaargh—heh!' business even louder, and dangling the dangerous toasted offering from one thumb and forefinger, while fanning her open mouth frantically with her free hand. Ty got her a cup of water, which she gulped back urgently.

'Thanks, babe,' she gasped, moving, inexorably, back to the television.

'You know those things need to be laid down on a fire proof mat for three hours before you should try to eat them, don't you?' muttered Ty, but she just laughed and ate some more, with little moans and shrieks of pain. She clearly liked Pop Tarts a great deal.

Ty winced as she turned up the volume on the morning's magazine programme. Between the features on radical surgery to remove unwanted fat and extraordinarily easy phone-in competitions for Spanish holidays, there was occasionally a bit of news. As he poured out his cornflakes, the glamorous girl reading it told him about a disastrous drought somewhere in Africa, sixty sailors still stuck under water in a submarine, running out of air, a pop star having a baby (still), the latest house prices and a cat called Lucky who'd travelled up and down the country for a week trapped under someone's car bonnet.

'. . . But fortunately for Lucky, her luck was in, and she was found by a car mechanic, just in the nick of time,' cooed the newsreader. 'And she's still got eight of her nine lives left! That's Lucky for you!'

It was intensely irritating. Ty thumped his cereal bowl onto the table and put his thumb right through the foil cap on the milk bottle, pushing too hard on it. Lucky?! Lucky to get stuck on a burning hot engine, travelling a thousand kilometres by motorway without food or water for a week? What was *lucky* about that?! Like his mum insisting he was lucky to have his teeth fixed so he could be handsome by the time he was 18. What was lucky about having teeth like his in the first place? And why, for that matter, was he so lucky to have Aunty Dawn being so *flexible* around him. Why couldn't his *mum* have tried to be a bit more flexible this time, and taken a day off for him?!

The only bit of luck he'd had since last Christmas was getting to go out to the Croft with Sam and maybe finding that interesting metal thing. It clunked in his school-trousers pocket, where he'd transferred it from his jeans. He got up again with an exasperated snort: he'd forgotten the spoon. With annoyance he got the spoon from the drawer noisily and slammed it down on the table, where it began to spin. He went to pick it up and then paused. It was *still* spinning. For much longer than he would have expected. Round and round it spun, quietly, balancing on the thin metal bridge that sat proud between the bone handle and the steel, barely making contact with the table.

After another thirty seconds, Ty was fascinated. How much longer would it spin? Stop it! he thought, suddenly. Cut it out.

Abruptly, the spoon stopped. Dead still. As if it had never been moving. Ty felt a pulse of shock and excitement pass through him. He held his breath. In his head a quiet, wary suggestion formed. *Spin again* . . . it whispered. And slowly, smoothly, the spoon began to turn, round, round—a full circle—picking up speed now—faster and faster. Ty felt his eyes bulging in his head and his breath coming more quickly. It was moving on its own! How was this happening? What was going on? The spoon was now spinning so fast that it began to sing – vibrating through the wooden table with a resonant moan which rose in pitch as the thing got faster and faster.

'What's that noise?' murmured Aunty Dawn absently, over her shoulder. Ty glanced up at her and immediately the spoon began to slow down and wobble to a halt.

Taking a shaky breath, the hair on the back of his neck standing on end, Ty reached out and dabbed at the spoon with his finger, and then harder, flipping it over. It felt warm and was vibrating very slightly. He sat back in his chair and stared at it. Perfectly still now, it reflected his startled face—upside down—back at him. OK, thought Ty, leaning forward again and resting his elbows on the table. Now—*move*. Nothing happened, although the metal of the spoon seemed almost to flicker at him. Silently, not moving his eyes from it, Ty raised his

22

finger and pointed to the left. The spoon slid smoothly to the left. Biting his lip to stop himself bursting out with excitement, Ty flicked his finger back to the right and the spoon skidded to a halt, turned neatly and then slid back to the right until it hit the breakfast bowl with a chink.

Ty looked around him for some evidence of trickery. He had seen those television shows where a camera crew hides itself in an ordinary home and then the technical people set up an elaborate joke with blind wire and magnets and hidden speakers and stuff, and then everyone watching cracks up laughing at the poor dope who falls for it when his cat starts talking or his chair starts floating or—or—his spoon starts obeying his thoughts . . .

But no cheesily grinning presenter leaped out from behind the fridge and revealed that he was on *Up For a Joke* or *Camcorder Disorder*, and chuckling that Aunty Dawn had helped the team to play a big trick on him for the people at home. Nothing happened at all, except that Ty sat in his chair, staring at his spoon like it was an alien.

After more than a minute in this trance, Ty shifted his gaze to the mug beside the cereal packet. He squinted at it and thought 'Lift! Lift up!' and the mug wobbled a little on its base, as if it were trying really hard to do as it was told. But that's as far as it got. Ty relaxed his squint and moved his stare to a fork on the side by the sink. This was more successful. It slid along as it was bidden and plopped wetly into the tea-stained water at the bottom of the washing up bowl.

'What are you *doing*?!' howled his aunt and Ty fell off his chair. Scrambling to his feet, he realized that she had never shifted her gaze for one moment from the TV. She was shouting at someone on the screen who had just guessed that the capital of France was Norwich, on one of the ridiculously easy cash prize quizzes.

Ty picked up the spoon and hit himself hard on the nose with it. Tears sprang into his eyes and he accepted that he really *was* awake. He realized that he should be going to school now, so he shouted a goodbye to his oblivious guardian and, grabbing his bag, ran out of the house. His feet automatically took him along the usual streets. His head was spinning. And his heart was expanding and contracting like a possessed accordion. One moment he was filled with such elation that he seriously considered trying to fly—and next he was squashing the feeling up like an empty plastic bag, trying to contain it and telling himself that he *must* be mistaken. People couldn't make things move just by looking at them. It couldn't be done. And if it could—why him? And why now? What had changed?

It was as he reached the school gates and joined the milling crowd of unenthusiastic pupils wandering in, that he thought about the thing he'd found at Kestrel's Croft and felt it thud again in his pocket. Perhaps *that* was it? Maybe he'd found—

'OI! Metal Mouth!'

Something hit the side of his head, hard. Ty was jolted back to reality by one of Dom McGill's frozen chicken fists.

Dazed, he staggered, and peered at Dom as if he couldn't remember who he was. Dom was sitting up on the gatepost near the school entrance and had swung his fist down as soon as Ty got close enough. On the other gatepost was Rod who was trying to kick him, but not quite succeeding because his legs were too short.

'You won't get away from us today, Metal Mouth!' hissed Dom menacingly as Ty moved on, rubbing his ear, which had taken the full brunt of the smack.

'Metal Mouth! Metal Mouth!' shrieked Rod, nasally. 'You're gonna get a—kickin'…'

He'd been trying to work out a rhyme for 'mouth' for the last five minutes without success.

'Why do you do that?' Ty heard Dom demand, annoyed. 'Stop trying to make up poems, you dipstick. It dunt even rhyme!'

'Nah – but it's blank verse, innit?' protested Rod, embarrassed. 'Anyway—it's all in the rhythm.'

'You are such a *girl*.'

Ty found it almost impossible to concentrate that day. Not because Dom and Rod and a handful of other 'casual' bullies were planning to severely injure him at 3.15, but because of the spinning spoon and the sliding fork. I can *move things*, he told himself, again and again. I can *move things with my mind!* Several times he pulled out the lump of metal or rock and stared at it, trying to find a clue to what was going on. Eventually he had to stop himself, or he was going to end up getting it confiscated.

Something was stopping him trying again. There were any number of things he *could* move. His pens and pencils; the globe; a text book. All of these things his eyes selected, ready for another go. But partly through fear of it *not* happening, and the depression that would then flood into him, and partly through fear of what else *might* happen, Ty kept his mind *un*focused, and delayed the moment again and again.

And of course, his concentration was also being severely hampered by Dom and Rod and their mates. At every opportunity, one of them bashed into him, shoved him, kicked his bag around the room under everyone's desks, threw paper pellets into his hair and endlessly, endlessly, muttered *Metal Mouth* or *Scrap Gob* or *See you at three-fifteen, Brace Boy.* He was staggered that none of the teachers picked up any of this. But teachers can sometimes be very distracted and some of them prefer it that way.

By mid afternoon, Ty was beginning to feel feverish. He couldn't wait to get out and try his mind out again; couldn't wait to get his beating over and done with, if that's what it took, just to be alone somewhere with his new power, to try it out, to test it and practise it.

The clock seemed to have been stuck between 2.30 and 2.45 p.m. for ever. He longed for it to be 3.15. He *had* to get out. Ty stared hopelessly at the big grey school timepiece on the wall as Mr Lowther droned on and on about the Tudors and Stewarts and their poor sanitation. Suddenly his eyes widened in amazement. The clock was *speeding up!* The minute hand was shifting quickly around the face, skipping past quarter to, up to the hour, whizzing down to ten past . . . Ty glanced around at the class but nobody else seemed to have noticed. Leaning over so that he could see through the window into the opposite class, Ty saw that its clock was moving on, too. They must all be connected. As the minute hand swept down to quarter past three a shrill bell sounded and everyone jumped.

'Good grief!' spluttered Mr Lowther. 'Time *does* fly when you're doing Henry VIII!"

The whole school was getting to its feet. Ty remained seated, glancing around him in amazement. Was nobody even questioning for a moment what had happened? Wasn't anybody going to shout out—'Hey! That can't be! It was half an hour ago, just five minutes ago!'

But nobody did. Children filed out, chattering happily, teachers packed up their books and papers and wiped down the chalkboards. Every one of them behaved as if it were the most normal thing in the world. Checking his wristwatch, Ty could see that time itself hadn't sped up (and was fairly relieved at this), it *was* just the clocks.

Everyone piled out to the gates just the same. Everyone headed out into the hazy afternoon sunshine and made their way home to empty houses, because mothers hadn't returned from shopping, or to the junior school to meet younger brothers or sisters who hadn't been let out yet. By the time the teachers worked out that the clocks had gone wrong, it was too late. The children had had an unexpected free period.

And for Dom McGill and his posse, there was much more time for pulverizing Metal Mouth. They had hared outside the moment the bell rang, and Ty, resignedly, made no attempt to catch them up or outrun them. He took his time and collected his coat in the wake of most of the school.

He knew it was probably pointless; there were just too many of them, but he squeezed out through a hole in the fence, away from the main gate, and made some attempt to run down a different road, changing his usual route. After a minute, he was surprised that there were no shouts and footfalls behind him and he slowed enough to glance over his shoulder. Nobody was following him. Uneasily, he slowed to a walk.

Looping back round towards his home, Ty reached the conclusion that Dom and Rod and company had found someone else to beat up. After all, he wasn't the only one they went after. There were half a dozen kids, small or fat or clever or just unfortunate, that regularly got thumped. Perhaps one of his unhappy counterparts had wandered across Dom's path. Relaxing, he allowed himself a small grin of excitement and squeezed the metal rock thing in his pocket. Soon, he told himself, soon. He walked up the alley at the back of the houses and turned the corner onto his patch of wild ground. Then he stopped. Scattered across the rough grass and nettles, holding sticks and lumps of brick, stood four boys, smiling meanly.

'Hello, Scrap Gob,' said Dom.

Chapter 4

'Did I hear people screaming?' asked Aunty Dawn, absently, when he got home. She was in exactly the same position she had been in that morning, sitting on a high stool, leaning on the draining board, watching the little TV in the kitchen. Teddy Taylor again. Today her snack of choice was Italian breadsticks. She was gnawing through them like a beaver in a pink jumper.

'Just some kids,' said Tyrone, dropping his school bag under the coats. If his aunt had looked at him, she would have seen his face was flushed and his eyes glittered as if he had a high temperature. Ty was in shock. He could still see the lumpy face of Dom McGill, as it shifted from the mean, excited anticipation of a good beating session to confusion and then alarm and then absolute terror.

When Ty had realized that his way home was blocked and there was no hope of outrunning them, he'd reached instinctively into his pocket for the rock thing. His heart went into a mad, haywire beat and he could clearly hear his own blood pulsing in the veins through his ears. Any minute now, he was going to get the worst thumping of his life. It was the first time Dom and his posse had looked this serious. Ty's quick brain skittered around all remaining possibilities—too late to run; no point in shouting for help; asking nicely *not* to be hit was similarly futile.

And then it happened. A cool *grey* sort of curtain slowly slid over his mind. Instead of blocking things out, it seemed to make them very much sharper and clearer. He could see Dom beginning to move towards him and Rod jumping from foot to foot, holding his bit of wood like a tennis player waiting for a serve. The others, too, were breaking into a swift trot, closing in on him. Ty focused on the things they were carrying and sent a sort of *pulse* out through his mind towards these objects. It seemed to push through the base of his skull, down his spine and into his solar plexus, just below his rib cage, and *out* towards them in a cool, swift, shivery wave.

Suddenly, Dom McGill hit himself in the face with his lump of brick. He gave a surprised yelp of astonishment and pain and stumbled to a halt just a metre or two from Ty. Rod stared at him like he'd gone mad. 'Watchoo doin' you spaz?' he said. And then he clouted himself on the ear with his stick. Well, actually, thought Ty—his arm didn't make the move. The stick did. It just launched itself up and whacked at Rod stoutly—but Rod's fingers were caught out and hadn't let go of the end of it.

The other two also began to attack themselves. Bill Smethwick smacked himself sharply in the nose with a vicious upswing of his club; Mike McCrony caught his lump of concrete on the chin. The air was suddenly filled with howls of pain and bewilderment. Everyone dropped their weapons and looked around at each other with amazement and dawning fear. Ty folded his arms across his chest and *pulsed* again and all of the weapons suddenly shot up into the air and hovered exactly fifteen centimetres above the aghast faces of each of his would-be assailants.

A thin wail rose up from Rod. 'I—dooooooooon't like it!' he informed his mates. They didn't like it either. They were staggering back now, desperately trying to put some distance between their heads and the silent, floating menace in the air above them, their frightened squeals and moans getting louder. 'Geddit off me! Geddit *off* me!' squeaked Dom, turning away from his brick and falling over an abandoned pram. Ty smiled and dropped the brick to within five centimetres of his shoulder. 'It's gettin' me! It's gettin' me,' sobbed the boy, crawling through the lumpy grass. 'Help me! Help me! Help!' He gave a scream like a passing express train and fell headfirst into Ty's secret culvert. His mates didn't hang around to help. Shrieking and choking and convulsed with terror, they were running past Ty back towards the alleyway. Mike McCrony shoved Rod so hard the boy slid, face first, into the dirt and then Bill Smethwick ran over his leg. Ty rapidly sent their weapons into a Red Arrows formation and cut them off just before they reached their escape route. The sticks and bricks hovered, bouncing up and down like excited gnats. They all stopped and backed up again, Bill stepping back onto Rod's leg, and then shrank down and down until they were all huddled in a desperate, sobbing heap.

From behind him, Ty could hear Dom McGill whimpering in the culvert. He decided he'd had enough. He sent the sticks and bricks up into a spectacular synchronized loop the loop and then dropped them all on a patch of thistles two metres from the quivering heap of boys. A cloud of dust and thistledown rose in the silence that followed the thud.

Ty took a sharp breath and shouldered his bag. 'See you tomorrow then, lads,' he said cheerily, and went home.

Ty raced his battered mountain bike faster than it had ever gone before, thrumming its tyres in a whirl across the hot afternoon streets towards Kestrel's Croft. He'd changed into jeans, trainers and a T-shirt and left the house at a run, without bothering to check in with Aunty Dawn. She hadn't yelled after him, so he guessed she was unconcerned.

In his pocket the rocky thing felt warm. It had been glowing again when he'd looked at it back in his bedroom, as if energized by all the action on the waste ground. There'd been no sign of any boys when Ty looked out across it from his bedroom window.

Ty's bike skidded to a halt by his usual lamppost and he leaped off it, slinging the lock on at great speed and snapping it shut, before hopping across the low wooden boundary to the nature reserve and sprinting into the wood. When he crashed into Sam's bungalow, five minutes later, he could hardly speak. Dripping with sweat, he babbled incoherently at the surprised ranger, waving something in his face and struggling to breathe.

'Ty! Slow down! Slow down! What the heck are you on about?' Sam flapped his hands at him and then seized him by the shoulders and shoved him onto his threadbare couch. 'Sit!' he commanded. 'Shut up! Breathe! In—out! In—out! Remember?!'

Ty took in large, shuddery breaths and felt suddenly exhausted. He flopped back into the corner of the couch, dislodging some little see-through tubs of dead spiders from the arm, and gradually got himself under control. He fished in his pocket for the rock thing and then held it out in his trembling palm, for Sam to inspect. Bemused, Sam picked it up and turned it around in his fingers. It was still glowing, although not so strongly now.

'What's this?' he asked.

'I don't know,' gulped Ty. 'But I think it's some sort of magic thing.' Sam shot him a sceptical look and shook his head. 'No, listen Sam!' said Ty, sitting up urgently. 'Stuff has been happening. Weird stuff. *Really* weird. Ever since I got that thing last night.'

'Wait,' said Sam, putting down the rock on the arm of the sofa and disappearing into his kitchen. He returned with a can and two glasses. Opening it with a click and a hiss, he poured them both a brown, bubbling measure of cold cola. 'I think you need the sugar—and I've a feeling I'm going to need it too.'

Ty took a couple of gulps and felt the drink coursing through his system almost immediately. The very action of doing something as ordinary as drinking cola made him feel better. He took a few calming breaths and then told Sam everything that had happened since last night. When he'd finished, concluding with the ragged heap of terrified boys cowering in the waste ground, he watched Sam for his reaction. Sam's face was impassive as he sat in the armchair across from him. He leaned across, picked up the rock thing and handed it to him, without a word. Then he sat back, drained the last of his cola and raised his eyebrows at Ty. He didn't say he didn't believe him. He waited.

Ty closed his fingers around it and once again seemed to feel it *nestle* into his palm. He closed his eyes briefly and then opened them to focus on one of Sam's many little tins, containing stuff which would put the average girl of Ty's age into a screaming fit for a week. Obediently, the tin rose a few centimetres into the air and hovered there. Sam's eyes bulged and he put down his glass with a clatter, sitting forward and staring at the tin as it performed a little dance for him and then sank, daintily onto his armrest.

'Holy manure!' whispered Sam. He blinked and then stared across at Ty. 'This is amazing. Amazing!' He sank back into his chair again, rubbing his mouth and staring at the tin. He'd gone a little pale, Ty noticed, beneath his year-round outdoors tan. Sam suddenly sat up again and seized the tin, turning it over in wonder and then held out his hand to Ty. 'May I?' he asked, and Ty handed over the rock thing. Sam took it carefully and closed his fist around it, staring hard at the tin. After several seconds, nothing happened.

'Nope,' breathed Sam, more with relief than disappointment, it seemed. 'I can't make it float.'

'Perhaps it takes a bit of time,' said Ty, helpfully. 'I mean, I had that thing with me all night. Maybe you sort of need to boot it up for a few hours.'

Sam shook his head. 'No. I don't think so. But we'll see. Ty . . .' he handed the thing back and looked at Tyrone seriously. 'Ty, this could mean a lot of trouble for you. I don't want you to think I'm sorry you found it—this *is* amazing. Utterly amazing. But . . .' He paused and shook his head. 'It's not much of a secret now, is it? Just a few hours after getting this . . . power . . . you've managed to freak out at least four witnesses. Very hostile witnesses. And was anyone else watching from a window? It's not good news. Not at all. People don't cope well with anything new or threatening. And you've suddenly got threatening.'

Ty bit his lip. He hadn't really thought about all this.

Sam was thinking hard. 'When you go back home, and go back to school tomorrow, it's vital—*vital*—that you don't talk to anyone else about this. And if any of those lads show up, you have to treat them like a mental case if they start babbling on about it. Do you understand?

Pretend you don't know *what* they're talking about. The only thing on your side is that this all sounds so preposterous, most people will simply not believe it. The downside is that there are *four* boys who will be coming out with the same story. Four. Damn, damn, damn . . .' Sam tailed off, worriedly. He rose and walked about in his untidy bungalow, stepping over and around the many boxes and branches and nests instinctively, tapping the tips of his fingers together.

Abruptly, he turned to Ty. 'Look—I've got stuff to do,' he said, suddenly brisk and businesslike. 'You need to go home and act normal. I need to think. Don't— *don't* say anything to your aunt. Maybe we'll talk to your mum when she gets back. When is she back?'

'On the weekend,' said Ty. 'I think.' He stood up, reluctantly. He'd been hoping to go off with Sam for a walk and try out lots of games with the rock thing. 'I'm going to call it Miganium,' he said, suddenly, rocking it in his palm. It glinted back at him, happily.

'OK,' said Sam. 'Miganium sounds fine.' He cupped his hands across his mouth and blew into them nervously, before tucking them under his armpits and resuming his anxious ambling around the floor. 'But you promise you won't use it again? Not until we meet again tomorrow? Promise me?'

'Sure! Fine!' said Ty. 'I'm not a kid, you know!' He tucked the Miganium carefully back into his pocket and headed for the door. 'See you tomorrow,' he called back to Sam. Sam nodded, absently. He was sitting on a rare bit of space on the floor, leafing through a small red book with one hand while rooting around under a pile of ancient bark and dragging out his old black phone with the other.

As he left, Ty heard Sam dialling and wondered if he were calling the police or something. He dismissed the idea immediately. If there was anyone he trusted in this entire world, it was Sam.

When he pedalled back up the path to his shed, Aunty Dawn was leaning out of the kitchen window, waving at him. She had the phone in her hand and was making violent jabbing motions at it, grinning, and nodding encouragingly. He deduced that someone had called for him, and, leaning his bike against the shed, went indoors.

'No! No, really? That's *fab!*' Aunty Dawn was saying, as he arrived in the kitchen. 'That's brilliant!' She paused to lick her fingers with a delicate slurp. Ty tilted his head to one side, trying to work out what she was doing. On the worktop he noticed an opened syrup tin and a spoon, leaking a golden pool across the draining board. 'So when is it? Wow! No—you'll just have to go out and buy stuff! Hey girl—you'll have the money now!' Aunty Dawn went for another excited lick, pressing the phone to her ear with her free hand. Ty wondered when she was going to get around to handing it over to him. He leaned against the doorway and tried to get his mind off the Miganium.

'Mmm—mmm—s'OK. He's here now. You can tell him,' said Aunty Dawn, and then handed him the sticky receiver.

'Hi,' said Tyrone.

'Hi, sweetheart. It's me!' Ty smiled. It was good to hear his mum's voice. He felt a rush of warmth and longed to see her again. Only a couple of days and she'd be giving him a hug and telling him that whatever it was, it would be OK. 'How are you doing, honey?' said his mum, and she sounded slightly edgy, with a higher pitch to her voice than normal. Ty's warmth began to cool. 'I'm fine, Mum,' he said. 'How's it going on the ship?'

'Good, good ...' she was definitely working up to something. Ty suspected he wouldn't like it. 'Sweetheart—I've been offered another job.' Ty felt a momentary flash of relief. Suddenly he pictured his bright, glamorous mum in a library, wearing a nice dress and glasses, checking in people's books, looking things up on computers, and always, *always* within reach. Just up the road and home for tea every day. 'Ty? Can you hear me?'

'Yes—go on,' said Ty, the image fading fast.

'It's on another ship,' she said, and Ty nodded glumly, the receiver bonding to his ear with syrup. 'It's a really posh one—five star. They had this singer booked and then she went down with shingles—and they needed a replacement, and they want *me!*' Ty nodded, as if she could see him. 'Congratulations, Mum,' he said, limply. 'When do you start?'

'Well, sweetheart, that's the thing. I *have* started. I'm, kind of, at sea now. I'm calling you from Gibraltar—well, just off it. Isn't that exciting?'

'So,' said Ty, trying to keep the lump in his throat from squashing his voice up high, 'so you're not back this weekend, then?'

'No, baby. I'm sorry.' And she did sound sorry. Not that it made any difference. 'I really am. I was looking forward to a hug from my best boy. And to seeing how your teeth are looking,' she added, enthusiastically. 'Ty, I know it's hard on you, and I'm so proud of you for taking it so well. But it's *such* a good opportunity. They're paying me bucket-loads—and when I get back we'll have a fantastic holiday together. Just you and me, before you go back to school.'

41

'Before I go back to school?' echoed Ty. 'I haven't started the holidays yet. I—hang on. How long is this cruise?'

She paused a moment, and then said, quietly. 'Six weeks, honey. I'll be seeing you at the end of August.'

'Right then,' said Ty, and this time he didn't bother to keep the tears out of his voice. 'Enjoy yourself. I'll see you later.' He heard her calling his name as he shoved the phone back at Aunty Dawn and ran upstairs, furiously scrubbing at his eyes and his sticky ear. Slamming his bedroom door, he flopped back hard onto his bed and stared at the ceiling, biting at his lip and letting the tears trickle down on either side of his face until they soaked into his pillow.

The picture of her, which he kept by his bedside and said goodnight to every evening, flipped up into the air and slapped its face into the wall. 'Sorry, Sam,' mumbled Ty, miserably. 'Couldn't help that one.'

Chapter 5

There wasn't a single murmur of Scrap Gob or Metal Mouth when Ty got into class the next morning. It was very quiet indeed, and three of the desks were empty.

'Seems like we've got a touch of the plague,' said Mr Brading. 'Dom and Rod *and* William, all off with it.'

But, in the far corner of the room, was Mike McCrony. As Tyrone walked to his desk the boy shrank down into his seat, his frightened eyes like saucers, and his fist screwing up some workbook paper in a spasm of nerves. Remembering Sam's advice, Ty gave him a look, as if he was nuts, and then sat down and turned to his books. It wasn't a comfortable lesson. As well as the tension seeping across onto the back of his neck from the petrified boy behind him, Ty had to bear Mr Brading, intent on being *funny* again. The whole class tittered wearily to order. You could tell when you were supposed to, because Mr Brading had a habit of tossing his pencil up into the air every time he thought he'd made a particularly clever remark.

The girls at the front were the best at it, some of them even managing a bit of a grin (it seemed that Mr Brading was convinced they all had crushes on him: he was wrong), but it was hot and muggy and only two days until the end of term. Nobody could really be bothered.

'You see, Romeo was really in love with the *idea* of being in love,' Mr Brading proclaimed. 'He was wandering around in a daze, gawping at the object of his desire from afar. Like most of you when the ice-cream van pulls up at break.'

They managed another lacklustre chortle and Ty fought down the urge to catch that irritating pencil with his mind as it spun up over Mr Brading's head, and poke it up the man's left nostril. The ice-cream van, as if brought in on cue by Mr Brading, did indeed pull up at that moment, with a warped and tuneless jangle which was meant to be a bit of Italian opera. Everyone jumped and Mike McCrony nearly fell off his chair and gave a terrified squeak.

'What *is* the matter with you this morning, Michael?' demanded Mr Brading, exasperated. 'You look as if you've seen a ghost. Are you ill, boy?'

Mike nodded and said, feebly, 'I feel a bit sick, sir.'

'Off to see the school nurse then,' said Mr Brading, hurriedly, clearly having no desire to see this proven to him.

The bell rang for break at that point and everyone trooped out behind Mike, who scurried away, with a panicky glance over his shoulder at Tyrone, in the direction of the school nurse's room. 'How does it feel, then, McCrony?' Ty found himself murmuring, under his breath. 'Not nice, is it? To keep ducking away from people because you're scared of what they might do to you.'

He squeezed the Miganium in his pocket and felt the warmth from it as he was swept along in the stream of pupils, heading out towards the ice-cream van and the playing fields.

Maths, which followed, was easier. Partly because Mr Carpenter was making no attempt to be a stand-up comic, but also because Mike McCrony did not return from the school nurse. Tyrone was just beginning to relax, absorbing himself in shapes and angles and degree measurements, when there was a knock at the door and an older pupil came in with a note for Mr Carpenter. He read it quickly and then beckoned to Ty. 'Tyrone Lewis—the head teacher wants to see you,' he said, without interest. 'Get on down to his study now.'

Tyrone got up and walked quickly out of the room, feeling slightly dazed. What could it be? Had Dom and his posse told on him? But who would believe them if they did? Ty felt his insides fizzing with anxiety as he knocked on the panelled oak door to the head's study.

'Come in,' said a voice, and Ty opened the door. Mr Barber was sitting at his desk, in a small office that smelt of old books and sugar paper. It was a typical school room, with pale green paint up to waist height, cream above it, and a graceless, metal-edged window which framed a view of the parched school playing fields. The head teacher looked similarly tired and worn, in his brown suit and wire-rimmed glasses. He smoothed back his sparse hair in a slightly nervous gesture and asked Tyrone to sit down.

'I've been hearing some rather strange things today,' he said, getting straight to the point. 'Three boys didn't come in this morning, and the one that did is being collected by his mother fairly soon. I've had calls from parents and a talk with Michael McCrony. They all seem to talk about the same thing. Something to do with a bit of a fight up behind Fitzhugh Lane on the wasteland. Boys getting hit with bricks and sticks and running home in a dreadful state. Do you know anything about this, Tyrone?'

Ty gulped. He *could* lie, but he thought it would probably be better not to. Four witnesses, after all, as Sam had reminded him, was pretty hard to brazen out. 'I saw *something*,' he said, carefully.

'Only,' went on Mr Barber, 'whatever *did* happen seems to have affected these boys quite badly—er—physically and emotionally. And, let's be straight here, Tyrone—Dom McGill and his friends aren't the type of pupils whom I'd describe as particularly sensitive, would you?' Ty shook his head, careful not to meet the head teacher's eyes. 'If I've got this right, these boys believe that there was some kind of *visitation* upon them. Something like a poltergeist. Do you know what that is, Tyrone?'

'Yes, sir. It's a spirit which chucks things about.'

'Hmmm. Well, apparently, there were sticks and stones hitting them, and they couldn't see *who* was throwing them. Does that make sense to you? Did you see sticks and stones?'

'I saw them all *holding* sticks and stones,' said Ty, truthfully. But he knew it was going to be hard to *stay* truthful.

The head nodded. 'And this *throwing about* of sticks and stones,' he prodded. 'Did you see that?'

'Stones and sticks *were* thrown,' confirmed Ty.

47

'And were you involved, Ty?'

'I had my hands in my pockets the whole time, sir. And after it got a bit out of hand, I ran home.'

'And you didn't get hurt?' Mr Barber asked, with a gentler tone to his voice. It was no secret that Tyrone was on the victim rota at his school. It was this that saved him. Ty carefully directed his eyes at the floor, fidgeted uneasily and mumbled, 'No sir. I was fine,' in a dejected, brow-beaten way.

'So that bruise on your cheek and the scratch on your arm were just accidents?' asked the head teacher, still with the same concern and gentleness in his voice.

It was quite touching to have someone pay him that much attention, thought Ty. Pity it had never happened after he actually *had* been beaten up. The scratch and the bruise were a result of last night's frantic dash through the woods to get to Sam. 'Yes, sir,' mumbled Ty in the same, small voice. 'I ran into a tree.' It was the absolute truth and it sounded like a giant whopper.

Mr Barber sighed. 'I see, Ty. I understand. Look— there are people you can talk to, you know. You can always go and see the school counsellor.'

'Yes, sir. Thank you, sir. May I go now, sir?' The head nodded resignedly and Ty got out of the room in seconds, amazed that he had managed an entire conversation about yesterday's mad events without once lying to the head teacher and without once giving away a *thing*.

When Ty knocked at Sam's bungalow door late that afternoon, he was feeling buoyant and excited again. He'd got around the awkward interview with Mr Barber and maybe that was that. Maybe Dom McGill and his cronies would just lay off him from now on and be too scared or embarrassed to say why.

Sam opened the door quickly. 'Hi. Come in. There's someone I want you to meet.' Ty was taken aback as he followed Sam into the sitting room. The last thing he'd expected was company. He badly wanted to tell Sam about the day's events and even more badly wanted to try out the Miganium again. But now Sam was introducing him to a small, skinny man, who wore a black zip-up cardigan and baggy black combat trousers. His dull brown hair was neatly parted and the thick lenses of his glasses made his eyes loom out of his pink face, magnified. There was a sticking plaster on his neck. A child's sticking plaster with a jolly bumblebee on it.

'This is Nathaniel Borage,' said Sam, with an absolutely straight face. 'He's an old friend of mine.' Dazed, Ty shook Nathaniel's slightly damp hand. He was about to say something polite when the man started motioning urgently at him to be quiet. His enlarged eyes stared wildly through their lenses, and he put one hand to his mouth while the other waved between him and Sam and then around the room. Then he silently mouthed 'Keep quiet!' and put on what appeared to be heavy black rubber gloves. Ty made a face at Sam, but Sam just bit his lip, looking only slightly abashed and shook his head, indicating that Ty should wait and see.

Nathaniel Borage let the cuff of the second glove go with a snap and then began to do a bizarre dance around the room, waving his hands up and down the walls and along the edges of the carpet, over the piles of books and nests and chunks of woodland matter, along the hems of the curtains, unsettling several large moths, and then, finally, up and down Ty and Sam. Ty was just beginning to think that Sam had gone barmy and joined a New Age religious sect which read people's auras or something, when Nathaniel finally spoke up. 'It's OK,' he said, in a nasal voice. 'You're clean. These are the best anti-bug gloves you can currently buy. Cost me a month's wages. There's nothing here. Yet.'

Sam breathed out loudly. 'That's a relief,' he said, slightly ironically.

But Nathaniel Borage gave him a hard stare. 'You cannot be too careful. Knowing what you know.' He managed to underline these words with such warning that Ty shivered. Ty opened his mouth to speak again, but before he could get one word out the weird Borage was at it again, whipping off the gloves and picking something up from the floor—a little gadget which looked like a bit of a car dashboard with its semi-circle of meter measurements and a red needle flickering across it. Nathaniel Borage pressed a button and the thing lit up and beeped at him. Then he turned to Ty and began to wave at him once more. Almost immediately the gadget started to whine. It was upset at his ankles, devastated at his hips and downright hysterical by the time it reached his head.

'Will you please give it a rest?!' snapped Ty, finally, swiping the thing away from him.

Borage stepped back and snapped the whimpering thing off, and blessed silence flooded back again. 'Off the meter,' he said to Sam, holding the thing out to him. Its needle had stopped, indeed, jammed right up to the right of the dial as if trying to break out. Borage grinned, suddenly, at Ty and the effect was quite alarming.

'Let's have a cup of tea,' suggested Sam. 'Pack up your gadgets, Nat, before the moths get in. Ty, come and help me.'

Ty quickly followed him out into his little kitchen. 'Sam—what the heck is going on? Who *is* that loony?!'

'I told you. Nathaniel Borage. Despite appearances, Ty, he's a highly respected writer and investigator of the paranormal and extra-terrestrial life. Look,' Sam grinned at Ty over the teapot, 'I know he's a bit barking, but actually he really *does* know his stuff. He's also into conspiracy theories in a big way, and he's an absolute authority on all that surveillance stuff. And I went to school with him, so I know we can trust him.'

'But why get him involved?!'

'Just . . . to be on the safe side,' said Sam.

They returned to the living room with the tea and found a place to perch among the clutter. Borage was still staring at Ty as if he was a dodgy lab experiment. After a while, Ty had to burst out, 'What?! What?!'

'Your readings showed extreme disturbance,' said Borage, matter-of-factly, dunking his digestive exactly three times, in perfect rhythm, into his tea. 'How old are you, Tyrone?'

'I'm thirteen. What's that got to do with anything?'

'Having a hard time at school?' He stretched his mouth wide, like a bespectacled frog, and carefully inserted the entire biscuit into it.

'No. Well . . . yes. But that's nothing unusual.'

'Hmmm.' Borage paused for a while, working the biscuit into pulp and then, after an abrupt swallow, resumed his questioning. 'Do things move around when you get angry?'

Ty considered this. Certainly that's how it had begun, he thought. 'Some of the time,' he said.

Borage nodded sagely and then said to Sam, 'Poltergeist.'

'I'm not so sure,' said Sam.

Borage picked up his meter gadget and switched it on again. A shriek spun out of it instantly and he snapped it back off again. 'I've never experienced an EMF reading this high. Except when I put it in the microwave once. This boy's magnetic resonance could reverse the poles.'

'Well, that's as maybe,' said Sam, patiently, 'but I don't think it's poltergeist activity. It's too controlled. Ty—show him.'

Pleased to be able to shove the cocksure paranormal whatnot off his perch, Ty pulled out the Miganium, squeezed it lovingly in his palm and zoomed in on the irritating gadget. Mindful that it was probably very expensive, he shot it high into the air and stopped it a few centimetres short of the ceiling. Then he spiralled it prettily down in front of Borage's eyes, which were now so stretched and huge he looked like the canary in the Tweety Pie and Sylvester cartoons. The gadget came to rest on the arm of his chair. To Ty's immense satisfaction, Borage was now staring at him in awe. He gulped and shakily took off his glasses and wiped them with a beautifully laundered handkerchief from his pocket. The deep purple indents on either side of his nose, where the heavy glasses normally rested, made him look slightly cross-eyed. He seemed to collect himself when he returned the spectacles to their resting place.

'This *is* extraordinary. The most convincing telekinesis I've ever seen,' he said. Ty handed him the Miganium and he scrutinized it carefully. 'What do you call this?' he asked Ty.

'Miganium.'

'Hmm—a made up name for an unrecognizable rock. Or metal. You're right Sam. It *is* like nothing we've ever seen. I'd say someone had made it, perhaps, but I don't know how they'd effect that glow, without an opening for power cells. It could be radioactive of course.' Ty and Sam looked at each other, startled. They hadn't thought about that. Borage calmly reached down to the black leather bag at his feet and extracted yet another piece of equipment. It was similar to the first meter, but chunkier and housed in bright yellow metal, with a carrying handle. Borage twiddled with a dial on the front and another meter twitched. The thing clicked gently, but not loudly or very fast. 'Hmmm,' he murmured. 'Only residual readings . . .'

'You mean there is *some* radiation?' burst out Ty, aghast.

'There's always *some*,' said Borage, disdainfully. 'Don't they teach you anything at school? But nothing to be concerned about—and no fluctuations at all, which perhaps bears out your theory, Sam, that this is not a poltergeist. Where did you find this—er—Miganium?'

'In the woods. The night before last,' said Ty.

'Anything unusual going on when you found it?'

'No. Nothing. Well—there was a bit of a summer storm.'

'Hmmm.' Borage pursed his lips and stared into the middle distance.

'Well . . .' prompted Ty. 'What do you think it is? A bit of lunar rock? Dropped by a passing astronaut or something? Maybe Buzz Aldrin was having a walk through the Croft and...'

'He may well have been walking through Kestrel's Croft,' said Borage testily, 'but there's no way he'd have dropped moon rock in it, seeing as he never laid his hands on any.'

'What?' Ty had seen the grainy black-and-white television pictures of the moon landings on a film at school.

'There *was* no moon landing,' said Borage, packing away his Geiger counter. 'It was all an elaborate hoax. The entire thing was filmed on a huge sound stage erected in a cave beneath the Nevada desert. Check the photos. No stars. Not enough dust. It was all a ploy to please the voters and upset the Russians.'

'Right,' said Ty, weakly. He looked at Sam, who was grinning and shaking his head.

Borage zipped up the bag and stood up, looking levelly at Sam.

'I think you both need to be very careful, Samuel,' he said. 'It'll be only a matter of time. Be prepared. And *you*,' he spun round and fixed Ty again with his odd, Tweety Pie eyes. 'If you see a man and a woman, in neat suits, walking towards you, do not wait to find out what they want. *Run.* Anywhere. Come here or go to a friend's place. Do *not* go to the police and do *not* go home. Is that clear?'

'Er—yes. OK,' Ty looked back at him, uneasily.

'The boy doesn't take me seriously,' said Borage, gathering his bag and walking to the door. 'You too, Samuel,' he said. 'You're in on this now. I doubt very much that you can contain it for long. You know where to find me. Call me if you need to but don't use your real name or your own phone. I don't know if I'll be able to help. Use your skills; they might help you more. Steer clear of cash points.' He glanced back at Ty and nodded curtly. 'Good luck, boy. And keep control.' And then he was gone.

Chapter 6

Ty slumped back into the corner of the couch with a blast of exhaled air. He mopped his brow and peered across at Sam, who had just done pretty much the same thing in the armchair opposite.

'Weird, I know,' said Sam. 'Very weird. But, truly, he does know his stuff.'

Ty shook his head. 'I don't understand,' he said. 'I just get this fantastic thing, this brilliant power, and all everyone can do is go all gloom and doom on me and start talking about Men In Black and stuff. Can't you just be pleased for me?'

Sam sat up. 'I *am* pleased for you, Ty,' he said. 'It's just amazing. But don't you see? People get very frightened around anything or any*one* that's different. It's why you've always been kicked about at school in the first place. You've always been different. Too bright for your own good and too quirky. Now, I happen to think you're great just as you are, but that's because I'm a bit quirky too, mate. The point is, now you're *more* different than anyone else I can think of, and it's dangerous. And I don't just mean getting bashed outside the school gates dangerous. I mean getting abducted outside the school gates dangerous. As soon as this gets out, there will be people—people with *authority*—who will want to find you and test you and work out if you're a threat to national security.' Ty gasped. 'Well—*think* about it. What are you capable of? Even you don't know that yet. You could turn this bungalow upside down. You could stop aircraft in the sky. You *don't know*.'

Ty felt a little sick. As if the power now humming through him *was* radiation after all.

'Ty—you're a good boy,' went on Sam. 'I know this. And I know you'd never do anything *bad* with the power you've got. But other people don't know that. What's more—you're a teenager. Teenagers aren't known for their steady, reasonable qualities. You're supposed to be growing hair everywhere and getting emotional about bands. A circus of hormones and sudden supernatural power are a dodgy combination even in *you*.'

'Well,' said Ty, slightly resentfully, 'there's nothing I can do about it. I can't *un*do this thing.'

'You could bury it,' said Sam, seriously.

Ty shot up out of the armchair. 'You must be joking!' he shouted. 'Anyway—it may not make any difference. Look.' He put the Miganium down in the far corner of the room and then walked to the door. Turning around he lightly picked up a book with his mind and spun it in the air for Sam to see. 'You see? I can do it now whether I'm holding the Miganium or not.'

'So you can,' whispered Sam. 'So you can . . .' He seemed lost in thought for a while, and then he snapped out of it and got to his feet. He went back into the kitchen and rummaged through a drawer. 'Look, Ty, in all likelihood, Nat *is* being over the top. He's always been a bit that way. Probably nothing will happen at all, especially if you keep your power under wraps. Just come out and have a go with it from time to time in the Croft, but *don't* let anyone else know. Except perhaps your mum . . . we probably do still have to warn your mum.'

'No need,' said Ty, remembering, with a dispirited sigh. 'Right now she's in the middle of the Atlantic Ocean, singing "Memory" from *Cats*.'

Sam put his head round the door. 'Seriously? Oh Ty, I'm sorry mate. It's happened again, hasn't it?'

Ty nodded and didn't say anything. Then he remembered his talk with the head teacher and relayed that to

Sam as the ranger carried on rummaging through the kitchen drawer.

'Well played, Ty!' called Sam, when he'd heard it all. 'So he just thinks it was a regular beating up that went a bit wild, does he?'

'Seemed to. I didn't really need to say anything. I didn't even have to lie. So hey – there *is* some benefit to being the geeky one that gets his head shoved down the school toilets.'

'That's good news,' said Sam, emerging from the kitchen with some small black and red things and some AA batteries. 'If he doesn't believe what they're saying it probably won't go too much further. Look – I finally found some batteries. Ty—here's a pager for you—and one for me. They're pretty basic; all they do is beep. They're connected to each other by radio frequencies. I used to use them around the Croft when I was working here with another guy. They've got a long reach—easily to your house or your school—and they're not on a mobile network.' He put the batteries in and tested the gadgets and they beeped discreetly. 'If—and I say *if* you see this fabled man and woman in suits, do as Nat says and clear out as quickly as you can—but make sure you hit this button on your pager. It'll set mine off and I'll go straight to the fallen oak down by the stream. OK?

I'll meet you there. And if you hear *yours* beep – you do the same. Get straight down there—doesn't matter where you are—make your excuses and leg it.'

Ty nodded. 'OK.'

'You haven't got a mobile, have you?' checked Sam. Tyrone shook his head. *Some* chance! 'Good – so we don't have to worry about that being traced, if Nat's conspiracy theory turns out to be the real deal. Look . . . it's probably just hot air. You'd better get back home and act normal again,' said Sam.

On the return journey through the woods, Ty began to think that Nathaniel Borage and his conspiracy theories had affected him. With every snap of twig and every sudden flutter of birds' wings he jumped. He had an oppressive feeling that someone was watching him the whole time and imagined cameras and suited operatives lurking in every tree and thicket. It made him angry. The Croft had always been somewhere he came to for relaxation; to get away from the world. Now it seemed like the world was getting into the Croft.

Back home, Aunty Dawn was still guarding her seat in the kitchen. Ty wondered why she never watched the big television in the lounge. Perhaps because it was too far away from the fridge. 'Hi babe,' she murmured warmly as he came in. This evening her snack of choice was popcorn. She'd already put away half an economy sized bag by the looks of things. From time to time the stuff caught at the back of her throat and she made noises like a cat bringing up fur balls. Ty regarded her plump back and rounded shoulders, clad in a purple jumper, and her fuzzy dark hair waggling slightly as she cheered on Teddy Taylor who was addressing the whooping audience on his talk show. *Talk* show?! Since when did anybody *talk* on Teddy Taylor? They bawled and shrieked, choked and cried and mostly tried to hit each other as they spilled their worst secrets out to the watching nation. Ty couldn't understand why anyone in their right mind would want to watch, but Aunty Dawn seemed to love it. Now the audience was chanting 'Te-ddy! Te-ddy! Te-ddy!' as if the man in the shiny suit and the dyed blond hair were some kind of god, and Aunty Dawn joined in, before she got some more popcorn stuck and started making the fur ball noises again. 'Oh—that man!' she sighed happily, when she'd recovered.

'I can't see it myself,' said Ty, getting out a tin of spaghetti to heat up. No chance of any 'real' food now for the next six weeks, he reminded himself, glumly. His mum was a good cook and tried hard to make up for her absences when she came home, by creating the most fantastic stews and curries and cottage pies with loads of fresh organic vegetables. Aunty Dawn let him have whatever he wanted from the cupboard. He supposed that now she would be doing the shopping for the next six weeks he'd have a wide range of popcorn, Pop Tarts and syrup to choose from.

Teddy Taylor had come to an end with a quick rattle of jazz saxophone music and a list of credits that flashed by so fast you'd have to record them and play them back in slow motion to ever be able to read them. Just as well, thought Ty. Who would ever want anyone to know that they worked on *The Teddy Taylor Show?* Now it was the news. Aunty Dawn groaned. She went to switch it over, but paused. 'Oh—those poor, poor men,' she said, sadly, and Ty looked up to see yet another report of the doomed sailors who were stuck underwater in the submarine that nobody seemed to be able to raise. '*What* a horrible way to go,' sighed Aunty Dawn heavily. 'Ooh! Ooh! Look—the baby!' she screeched delightedly, less than half a breath later, as the pop star who'd been having a baby appeared on the screen, leaving a posh London hospital with a bundle in her arms and beaming at the press in full make-up. When the news moved on to starving children and the political problems of the government in their country, Aunty Dawn had had enough and started flicking through the channels for reality TV shows. Anything but *real* reality.

Six weeks! thought Ty, desperately. Six weeks of Aunty Dawn in her constant state of stickiness, screaming at Teddy Taylor and blithely paying no attention at all to her nephew. 'Aunty, I've developed supernatural powers,' said Ty, conversationally. Aunty Dawn gave him a little wave over her shoulder. 'That's lovely, babe.' Ty sighed, finished the last of his spaghetti and went upstairs.

It occurred to him that if Sam was getting all prepared for emergencies, like giving him the bleeper thing, he should probably do something too. He emptied his school bag of all its contents and then put just a couple of things back in. Just one more day tomorrow and then it was the end of term anyway, so he doubted he'd need anything much. Feeling like a boy scout, being prepared, Ty pulled a pair of clean jeans and a sweatshirt, and a couple of pairs of underpants from his drawers. He rolled them up into a tight, compact bundle and stowed them at the bottom of his bag. He threw his trainers in too, with some socks rolled up inside them.

He dug around in his cupboard until he unearthed a box containing some of his treasures. There were several semi-precious gemstones which his mum had brought back from her trips abroad and a St Christopher pendant that had been his dad's. There was also a little cheap wallet with some cash in. Not much; a couple of notes and some coins, but Ty slung it in the bag anyway. He put the St Christopher around his neck. There was also a Swiss Army knife, which was always useful. He added that too, resisting picking it up with his mind, as he'd promised Sam he wouldn't. He'd have to add his toothbrush after he'd used it in the morning. He couldn't think of anything else, although, after a pause, he picked up the photograph of his mum, still leaning face-in to the wall since last night, and put that in too. It was probably all for nothing, and he'd just be weighed down with useless stuff tomorrow, but he might as well make an effort, *just* in case. He thought about Borage's 'man and woman in a suit' marching across the playground and had to laugh. It was the stupidest idea imaginable. He should probably take all that stuff back out of his bag now. He would, in the morning.

The next day was another gloriously sunny one and when he got up in the morning Ty very nearly did empty out all the stuff he'd packed the night before. With the birds chirping and the postman whistling, life couldn't have felt more normal or less threatening. But the Miganium was glowing again, warm in his hand, and he reminded himself that possibly nothing would ever be normal again.

Aunty Dawn was shuffling down the stairs in her robe and slippers, looking bleary-eyed and squashed from sleep. 'You know,' said Ty, hopefully, 'You don't actually *have* to stay here with me the whole time. I mean – you're only two roads away, and we're both on the phone and . . .'

'But I couldn't leave you here all on your own!' protested Aunty Dawn, reaching the hallway and bending down with a puff to pick up the post. 'What would your mother think of me? I'm your guardian!'

Ty snorted and then turned it hastily into a cough. He suspected that Aunty Dawn was actually much happier in his house than at her own cramped little studio flat. A nice try, but it wasn't going to work. He ate breakfast quickly and headed out before she could get the TV on. 'Have a good day, babe,' she called after him in a muffled voice, her head in the fridge.

At school, Mike McCrony hadn't returned, but Ty was surprised to see Rod back. He had a thick white bandage taped to his ear and a wild look in his eye when he saw Ty. Ty grinned and waved at him and he froze in his seat. Throughout the morning Rod said nothing and made not one sound. Considering he was the type to whinny like a hyena every time some fellow pupil struggled with reading aloud or answering a question, it was very odd. Several times, Ty's classmates peered around at Rod, trying to work out what was going on. Nobody was very sympathetic about his injured ear, and, without Dom's gang to back him up, he looked a pathetic, lonely figure.

During chemistry, a pupil came with another note from Mr Barber, but this time it was for Rod. Rod stared at the teacher and then at Ty for some seconds before getting shakily out of his seat at the laboratory bench. Ty watched him edge past, as far away as he could. When he reached the door, the boy broke into a scuttle and disappeared down the corridor. Mrs Wilson shook her head in wonder and then went back to her potassium permanganate.

For a while, with Rod gone, Ty slipped back into normality, tweaking the collar on his Bunsen burner and writing notes with Louise Campbell on the experiment they were sharing. The class was content and interested and Mrs Wilson was as light-hearted at the thought of six weeks' break as they all were. And it really was remarkable how much better everything was without Dom and the others.

With just ten minutes to go until lunch break, Rod returned, looking white, with dark rings under the eyes.

He handed Mrs Wilson a note and slunk back to his seat, peering at Ty fearfully. 'Oh dear—can't it wait? We're nearly done here!' Mrs Wilson muttered. As it was end of term it hadn't been a proper lesson anyway—just a few fun experiments. 'Oh well—Ty, the head teacher wants to see you now! Are you nearly finished?'

'Yes, we've done it all now, miss,' said Ty and Louise nodded.

'OK then—off you go. I don't suppose I shall see you again before the end of school, so have a good holiday.'

'Thanks Miss,' said Ty, heading out, anxiety creeping back across his shoulders. What could the head want now? He'd just been seeing Rod, hadn't he? Maybe Rod had convinced him about the flying sticks and stones after all. But surely he couldn't believe it?

Ty knocked on Mr Barber's door for the second time that week and heard the head say 'Come in,' once again. He shoved the door open and saw the man at his desk, looking as tired and worn as before, but also a little tense.

'Hello again, Tyrone,' he said and there was a definite edge to his voice. Ty couldn't work out what it meant. Mr Barber scored his middle fingernail repeatedly across his thumbnail in a nervous way and nodded to his left as the door swung shut. As Ty looked around he said, 'Tyrone – this is Mr Chambers and Miss Merrill from the local education authority. They want to speak to you.'

Sitting on the school's orange plastic chairs to the side of his desk were a man and a woman wearing neat dark suits.

Chapter 7

The woman smiled at Ty abruptly, revealing smudges of orange lipstick on her teeth. The colour clung to her thin lips, a stark slash in her long, colourless face. Her eyes were a very pale grey and her brown hair was done in a 1950s style. Her neat navy blue blazer was buttoned over a beige polo neck top, and her skirt was a matching blue with a starched hem that hung stiffly at an angle over her thickly-stockinged knees and sensible black slip-on shoes. The man was younger and also in a dark navy suit, more current in style. He had close cropped dark hair and wore small, round, rimless glasses which Ty suspected were just to make him *look* bookish, because he was well built and clearly athletic under his neat clothing.

'Ty—do sit down,' said Miss Merrill, sweetly. The forced pleasantness of her voice made Ty think of a posh damask tablecloth draped over a coarse metal and chipboard table. Mr Chambers said nothing, but his thumb repeatedly prodded the button on the top of his stainless steel ballpoint pen, making the nib pop in and out with little metallic clicks.

Ty's heart was racing as he sank onto the chair put out for him opposite them all. He felt the pager lying in his trouser pocket on the opposite side to the Miganium and wondered whether he dared to press it now. Trying to run at this moment seemed impossible, with his head teacher looking at him gravely and the two important people here to see him. And yet this was exactly what Borage had warned him about. A strange man and woman in suits, only they weren't walking towards him, giving him a chance to run. They had hidden themselves and snared him in with the help of the head teacher.

Even now part of Ty was arguing, *'Don't be daft! They're just school inspectors or something! You're not in some science fiction film, you idiot!'* But a different voice cut into these thoughts again, urging, *'RUN! Don't stop to ask. Just RUN!'* Ty trembled on the edge of his seat, wondering how quickly he could get the heavy oak door open and clear the end of the corridor outside.

'Don't be nervous, Ty,' said the woman, as if they were friends. People didn't generally shorten his name until they knew him quite well. 'We're just here to ask you a few questions—about the silly fight that happened near your house earlier in the week. We're sure it's nothing at all to worry about, but,' here she sighed and shrugged, tilting out her palms towards Ty as if asking for his understanding, 'sometimes parents demand some kind of action when their children get caught up in . . . high jinks, and we have to, well, tick a few boxes, to make them feel better. You understand?'

Ty nodded silently, his mind working furiously on escape routes. The window was open and he was pretty sure he could leap through it before they even got off their seats. Problem was, this room was on the second storey and he would probably break both his legs.

'Now then, about that fight,' Miss Merrill smiled at him again with her orange teeth. 'Mr Barber here thinks you were probably on the receiving end of some bullying. Is that right?'

'I have been,' muttered Ty, evasively. He wondered if he could lift *himself* with his mind power as he flew out of the window, and give himself a gentler landing. He doubted it.

'Apparently there were four boys—and yourself—on this piece of waste ground near your house. And then something a bit unusual started happening, with sticks and stones—*floating* in the air? Ty?'

Ty gave her a look that was meant to convey confusion and doubt over her state of mind. He saw her press her lips together tightly and a steely look came into her eyes. 'Ty—you did see something, didn't you? Boys getting attacked. By an unseen force. You saw something, didn't you? You had something to do with it, didn't you? Come on, now, don't waste my time.' Her voice was getting sharper and nastier with each syllable and Mr Barber got up from his desk, looking very uncomfortable.

'Now, look, Miss—er—Merrill,' he began, but she held up her hand in a sudden gesture of such authority that he was silenced, and sank slowly back into his chair, looking diminished and miserable. The man stopped clicking his ballpoint pen, slid it back into his breast pocket and stood up, walking behind Mr Barber's chair and leaning against the wall, folding his arms over his broad chest and saying nothing. Mr Barber wiped his brow with his handkerchief.

Of all the things that Ty had hoped might come to his rescue, he hadn't thought about his own innards. At that moment his stomach, churning in a frenzy of agitation, gave the most enormous gurgle, followed by a small, plaintive whine. Everyone blinked. 'Sorry,' said Ty, in a weak voice. 'I'm feeling a bit sick. I think it was the stuff I ate for breakfast.' They stared at him and

Miss Merrill pursed her nasty lips sceptically. Ty began to making heaving noises and pressed his hands over his mouth. He was sweating with fear and knew that it must look quite convincing. 'Can I just go to the toilet, please?' he mumbled through his fingers. Miss Merrill gave an exasperated sigh. 'Go on then,' she said irritably. 'But just five minutes please! Mr Chambers and I are on a very tight schedule.'

Ty leaped up from his seat and was out of the door and down the corridor in seconds. He sensed, rather than saw, that Mr Chambers had followed him out and was tailing him at a discreet distance. Ty tore down the concrete stairs past a flood of pupils who had just been released for lunch and turned the corner towards the boys' toilets. By good fortune his bag was on a peg in the corridor along his route and he snatched it without pausing as he ran past, slinging it over his shoulder.

He skidded into the boys' toilets and pelted down the far end to the one he guessed was his best option. This cubicle was slightly larger than the rest and often housed the caretaker's mop and bucket in one corner. The window in it was also slightly larger than the others. Ty prayed that it wouldn't be locked. As other boys clattered in, shouting and laughing and shoving each other against the doors, Ty climbed up on the cistern of the toilet and reached up to the small opaque window. He pulled up the grimy metal handle and it gave without a fight. A small blast of dust blew in as he tilted the glass outwards as far as it would go. Beneath the window was some paving and a small grassy strip which stretched over to some dense conifers planted along the school fencing, shielding the neighbours from the rear view of the bleak yellow-brick building. Sometimes kids came round to talk secrets or attempt to set fire to things, but happily, today, nobody was there.

Ty slung his bag out of the window and climbed up onto the sill. He was thankful that he was such a skinny boy as he wriggled out, feet first, grazing his hips and chest on the rough bricks outside the sill and then dropping down onto his feet and falling to a wary crouch. No way could Dom McGill have managed that. Ty caught his breath for only a second before grabbing his bag and pelting across to the cover of the conifers. He was certain he heard an adult male voice ring out curtly from the boys' toilet window—a voice asking if they'd seen *him*, no doubt. Ty scrambled along between the high chicken-wire fencing and the conifers until he reached a gap in the fence that he, and all the other boys on the victims' rota, knew well. The little hole torn through the criss-cross wire was a chance to get ahead of the bashing that was coming to you and maybe stave it off for another day. Ty ducked through and broke into a sprint down Coal Lane. As he ran he reached into his pocket and jabbed the button on his bleeper wildly, hoping it would work.

He tore along streets and lanes, past shops and factories, over wasteland and playgrounds and finally along the very edge of the housing estate which bordered Kestrel's Croft. As he reached the first few trees he heard a beep and realized that his pager was going off too. Perhaps in answer to his clumsy messaging to Sam. Ty nearly ran to the bungalow, in his panic, but remembered just in time that they'd agreed to meet up by the fallen log near the stream. He switched around and staggered on through the wood, oblivious to the fine branches and twigs that tore at his face and his school clothes and bag. When he reached the log he didn't see Sam at first, and then he felt something smash into his shoulder. Gasping, he turned in terror. It *was* Sam—but he wasn't stopping to talk. He gave Ty another urgent shove, holding his finger across his lips, and propelled him on across the stream, the cool water briefly invading his hot school shoes, and to the other side. In his exhaustion—he'd been running hard for fifteen minutes—Ty couldn't speak anyway, so they just ran on and on and on, Sam wrenching him to his feet every time he stumbled over a root or ditch and ruthlessly forcing him ahead, deeper and deeper into the Croft. After maybe another ten minutes of this, Ty was dripping with sweat and dizzy with the heat and the immense physical effort. At first his terror had helped him to run faster than he ever had in his life, but now it was weakening him. Why didn't Sam stop and talk to him—reassure him that everything would be OK? But Sam just kept shoving him on and on, panting and perspiring himself and wearing a look of such iron-clad determination that it never occurred to Ty to protest.

Finally, Sam hauled Ty to a stop. But just as he was about to slide to the ground Sam hissed 'No! No! Up!' Dazed, Ty looked above him and saw that there were rough climbing holds in the oak tree they had stopped under. Way up in the canopy, he could just make out some stoutly nailed-in boarding. 'Go! Go!' urged Sam, hauling him up by his shirt and launching him onto the tree trunk. Ty climbed the tree as fast as he could, his arms and legs trembling wildly with spent effort and his backpack weighing him down unbearably. Sam came up close behind him, driving him on. At last they reached the boards and Ty realized that it was a hide. A small wooden box, big enough to house three or four enthusiasts for bird or wildlife watching. He fell into it, snagging his wet cheek against the splintery floor and gasping for air. Sam staggered in behind him and immediately went to the narrow post-box windows to look out.

For a minute or two neither of them had the ability to speak. Sam sank into a corner and concentrated on breathing and Ty lay where he'd fallen, seeing tiny squiggles dancing in front of his eyes and wondering if he'd ever be able to walk again.

Eventually Sam gasped, 'Bungalow—done over. A mess. Everything wrecked.' Ty found it hard to imagine how anyone would *know* that Sam's bungalow had been done over and how even he could tell it was now a mess, but he was alarmed by the ranger's obvious distress, even in the midst of his own.

'But why?' he asked, aloud, struggling to sit up.

Sam shook his head forlornly. 'I don't know. It could just have been burglars, but the telly and the hi-fi were still there.' Ty looked at him blankly; he'd never *seen* a telly or hi-fi at Sam's. 'So it could be about *you*,' said Sam. 'About the Miganium. I don't know. It's just too much of a coincidence isn't it? And I guess something's happened to you too, or you wouldn't be here now. I got your bleep just as I was trying to decide whether to send you mine. What happened?'

Ty slumped onto the wall next to Sam, breathing more normally but still shaking. 'A man and a woman in suits,' he said.

'You're joking!' breathed Sam. 'Nat was right? After all these years . . . he was right.'

'I thought you said he was highly respected and all that, anyway?' said Ty.

'Oh—oh yes. Well, he is. But I have to confess, I *have* sometimes wondered about him. I mean there is no doubt that he knows his stuff, but I'd never seen anything to convince me he actually *knew . . . stuff*. Go on, then . . . what happened?'

While Ty told him of the events of that morning, Sam shook his head in amazement and concern. He looked impressed and amused when Ty told him about the being sick stunt and the escape from the boys' toilets. When Ty finished his story he abruptly began rooting through his backpack which, as far as Ty could make out in the gloom of the little wooden hide, was filled to the brim with gear. Expecting to see him unearth a compass or a bit of twine or a sheath knife, like he normally did, Ty was surprised and very pleased to see him pluck out another one of his cans of cola. He tapped it hard three times with his forefinger and then bent back the ring pull. The drink fizzed madly and shot up into the air like a geyser, but subsided quickly. Sam offered it to Ty who received it thankfully and took several long gulps before handing it back. Sam did the same and they both felt the intense hit of sugar helping them back to normality.

'What are we going to do now?' asked Ty, after a short silence.

Sam pulled a piece of paper out of his pocket. It was a print-out from a computer—some text which looked like a newspaper story. 'Find him,' said Sam, pointing to a picture of an elderly but robust looking man next to the writing. Ty peered at it, confused.

'I got an email from Nat late last night,' explained Sam, 'He'd been searching on the net, checking through all the on-line newspapers to see if anything odd had occurred which might help explain your sudden powers and the Miganium. He attached this, from this week's *Manchester Evening News.*'

Ty read the article.

HAVE A GO PENSIONER FOILS THUGS

proclaimed the headline. It went on:

Plucky OAP Bob Parker gave a gang of youths the shock of their lives when they tried to raid his home.

Bob, 71, from Burnside Avenue, didn't stand by when the six teenagers smashed his front door window and forced their way inside, but fought back with anything he could lay his hands on.

Police were called by neighbours who heard shouts and screams coming from Mr Parker's house, and, when they arrived, found all six alleged burglars still inside the building, too frightened to run away and surrounded by household appliances.

'It seems that the lads were severely frightened by Mr Parker actually standing up to them,' said investigating officer DC Brian Phillips. 'And it certainly is amazing that a man of his years could throw a television. When we arrived, they all came quietly and are helping us with our enquiries down at the station.'

Detectives last night had not yet charged the youths, but did not deny claims that a police surgeon and psychiatrist had to be brought in to treat them. Apparently the force of the counter-attack so shocked them that they thought they were in the presence by some sort of poltergeist, a neighbour told us, at the scene.

'They were shouting 'Get it off me! Get it off me!' said Maureen Stamp, 42, who lives next door to Mr Parker. 'And you've never heard so much screaming. They looked a bit of a state when they came out too, bleeding and messed up and one or two of them were definitely crying.'

Mr Parker is now being hailed as a hero by his long suffering neighbours who claim they have been terrorized for months by the youths now in custody. But, modestly, he refused to talk to our reporters about the incident.

Ty looked up at Sam in wonder. 'Do you think . . . ?'

'It could be, couldn't it?' said Sam.

'I don't know if *I* could chuck a television,' said Ty, in awe.

'You might, if you were angry enough.'

'So you think we should go and find him—in case he's got some Miganium too?'

'I can't think of anywhere else to go right now,' said Sam. 'Can you?'

Chapter 8

Even if Sam had owned a car he couldn't have driven them to Manchester. Sam went everywhere by train or by bike or by foot. He knew the woods across the South of England as well as most people knew motorway routes and owned a tightly bound sheaf of very fine, very expensive maps that charted the entire country's remaining wildernesses in great detail.

It wasn't that Sam was funny about people driving cars and polluting the atmosphere. It was that he was an epileptic. He'd revealed this about six months previously when he'd gone into what he'd called a *'petit mal'* in Ty's company. They'd been chatting animatedly one minute, about fungi and how to tell what was poisonous and what was edible, and Sam had been showing him a huge fan of reddish stuff on a tree, known as 'beefsteak' fungi, which could be stewed and eaten, when abruptly he'd stopped talking.

When Ty looked up Sam was motionless, staring into the middle distance. He swayed very slightly and the wind moved his collar, but he didn't speak. He looked as if he'd shut down, like a faulty robot. Ty was alarmed. He shouted Sam's name and Sam still stood there. Ty was just getting ready to shake him when, just as abruptly, Sam was back. He blinked, looked slightly confused, and then squinted at Ty as he stood staring at him. 'Oh, sorry,' he said, looking abashed. 'Did I go off?'

'Go off? Yeah—you went off line!' said Ty, shaken. 'What was *that* about?!'

'Did I say anything or do anything?' asked Sam, sitting down carefully and taking a few deep breaths.

'What?! You know you didn't!' said Ty, wondering if Sam was winding him up.

'No, Ty, I don't know. I was having a *petit mal*. It's a kind of mild seizure. I'm an epileptic.'

Ty was shocked, and felt guilty for being so dense. 'Oh . . . blimey! Are you OK? Should I put a cold spoon down your neck or something?'

He was relieved when Sam laughed. 'No—no cold spoons necessary! I'm fine. I very rarely have *petit mals* these days. Maybe once or twice a year. Very, very occasionally—about five times in my life so far—I've had a bigger seizure, where I black out. I go a bit loopy

85

beforehand apparently. But I think I may be past that now. I haven't had one for four years.'

He and Sam had talked some more, and Sam told him about not being able to drive or operate any heavy machinery. It was one of the reasons he'd gone into working outdoors for the county council in their wildlife havens. That, and the fact that he loved anything creepy, crawly, flappy and feathery.

Now, for the first time, Ty realized that Sam's condition was going to be a handicap. It was going to be difficult to get up to Manchester without a car. 'Have you got any money?' he asked Sam, digging out his own meagre fund, as they traipsed north across Kestrel's Croft in the mid-afternoon sun. 'We'll have to get a train or a coach or something.'

Sam pulled a thick, tightly curled wodge of notes out of one of the pockets in his ranger's waistcoat. 'I took out all I could get from the bank yesterday, just in case. I didn't really believe it would come to anything, but I just felt . . . like I should be prepared. I know Nat said not to, but we'll need it. We can't go to a cash point again though—they'll be able to track our movements through the banking system.' He stuffed the money back in securely. 'I don't think we should get a train yet— not around here. They may have people watching. We should keep hiking today. We can get right to the north of the county barely using the roads, and then maybe we'll get one from there.'

'I still can't believe this is really happening,' muttered Ty. 'Surely if I just went home, they couldn't just come and get me. Mum would—' he broke off and corrected himself. 'Actually, Aunty Dawn would be as much help as a butter bike. She'd probably hand me over in return for a Jaffa Cake. Should we contact her though, Sam? Do you think? She drives me nuts but she's all right really, and I wouldn't want her getting in a state and phoning Mum.'

Sam thought for a while. 'She may already know that you've run off,' he said. 'And if she doesn't it's only a matter of hours before she does. I suppose you could give her a call from the box on Stanton Lane—just say you've gone to stay for a couple of days with a friend. Do you think she'd believe that?'

'She might,' said Ty. 'And it might throw them off our scent for a bit. I'll say I've gone down to my mate Jim's in Devon. The one I met at a summer camp last year. I'll tell her she said yes. We have so many conversations when she just nods and waves and doesn't hear a word I say, she might believe that.'

They edged out towards the road that ran along the north eastern edge of the Croft and found the phone box.

'It's smashed, it's filthy, it smells of wee,' murmured Ty, opening the door with his nose wrinkled in revulsion. 'Check, check, check—everything's normal.' He picked up the receiver and was relieved to find that, against all his expectations, the phone was working. Aunty Dawn answered after two rings. The phone was close to the kitchen television.

'Ty! Where are you?!' she said, immediately, although she didn't sound as if she'd been pacing the floor tearing out clumps of hair with worry. 'The school rang to say you'd taken off at lunchtime! They wanted to know where you were.'

'Oh, Aunty!' sighed Ty, exactly as he'd rehearsed it in his mind. 'Don't you remember? I'm going to Jim's for the weekend! Like we said! You were supposed to call and tell my teacher I needed to get away a bit early for the train!'

There was a pause and then Aunty Dawn said, uncertainly, 'Was I? Did we say?'

'Yes!' said Ty, sounding exasperated but fond of her. 'Honestly, Aunty Dawn—I sometimes think you never hear me!'

'Well, I know I'm a bit scatty at times, love, but . . .'

'I told you last _week_—and again this morning—that Jim had phoned up to say could I come down to Devon for the first weekend of the summer holidays. I was packing my stuff last night and I said about it again this morning. Look upstairs—you'll see I've taken my toothbrush and I've even got mum's picture with me in my backpack!'

'Oh . . .' said Aunty Dawn. 'Sorry Ty—you're right. You *did* say! I'm such a dope! But how are you getting there? I didn't give you any money for the train!'

'It's OK,' said Ty, improvizing wildly, 'Jim's mum sent me the ticket last week. I've got it with me. I just got off at Paignton to give you a call to make sure you'd remembered and weren't freaking out because I wasn't back.' Fat chance of that, thought Ty. 'I'd better go soon because the train goes on again in five minutes. Do you want to write Jim's number down again?' She made pen-finding noises and Ty gave her Jim's number, taking care to change a digit in the middle of it, so it would seem like she'd just written it down wrong if anybody came to check later. Ty was feeling quite pleased with himself. He seemed to have thought of everything. As long as she didn't think as far back as yesterday, when he was so upset at his mum not coming home for the weekend, he was in the clear.

There was a worrying pause, but Aunty Dawn wasn't given to much deep thought. 'All right, babe. Well—I'll miss you. When are you back?'

'Sunday night,' said Ty, trying not to puff out in relief. 'But I'll call you, OK? So if you forget to call me it doesn't matter.'

'OK. Have a lovely time. Oh—and Ty—I nearly forgot. Some people were asking for you this morning.'

Ty's heart stood still. 'Who?' he croaked, while Sam peered anxiously through one of the broken panes of glass.

'Some school people I think,' she said. 'I think they were doing a survey or something. They wanted to know about extra-curricular hobbies and stuff that children in our area are doing. I told them all about your moth man and the naturist stuff you do . . .'

'Naturalist, Aunty, naturalist,' corrected Ty, slapping his forehead bleakly. 'Naturists are the naked people.'

'Oh—right. Well, anyway, they seemed really interested and said they might come back later to talk to you. Oh! That's a shame, isn't it?'

The pips began to go on the line. 'Sorry, Aunty. Got to go,' said Ty and hung up quickly. So it was Aunty Dawn who'd sent them right to Sam's place. He related the end of the conversation that Sam hadn't heard, and Sam gave a low whistle at Ty's story.

'First you play the head teacher and now you play your aunt!' he said, with an admiring chuckle. 'You should be a psychologist—or a con man!'

'Shouldn't you phone in to work?' said Ty, but Sam shook his head firmly and led the way back into the woods.

'I work for the county council, Ty, and the county council works for the government. I'm afraid there's no way I can talk to anyone safely. Not now.'

'But how do we even know those people *are* from the government? And if they're *bad* people . . . ?'

'We don't. Except that they seem to have the power to overrule your head teacher without any difficulty. And you tell me—did they *seem* good?'

Ty thought of Miss Merrill and her orange teeth and shuddered. 'No,' he said. 'They didn't.'

Another hour of walking took them out of the Croft, across some green fields and along a narrow belt of wooded land that skirted a stretch of motorway where they stopped for a rest. The rumble of the traffic was deadened by the thick canopy of green leaves above them and the optimistic chirping of the birds, content in spite of their never ending stream of fume-blowing, thundering neighbours.

Sam and Ty found a comfortable log and Sam emptied a packet of sandwiches from his backpack. 'Enjoy them,' he said. 'Bush tucker for tea.' Ty grinned, munching into the cheese and ham doorsteps hungrily. He'd eaten bush tucker with Sam before, on special woodsman weekends that he ran for people who wanted to learn survival tips. Sometimes it was weird and woody and sometimes it was fantastic. It depended what you could get. They washed their lunch down with water from Sam's battered metal flask and traipsed on through the late afternoon, clambering over many storm-felled trees and sometimes hacking through dense undergrowth with Sam's small, dependable axe, which he always carried on a hike. Ty had no idea where they were going, but could sense that it was north. He knew better than to question Sam. Sam undoubtedly knew exactly where they were.

Now that they were actively *doing* something about the bizarre situation he'd landed them in, Ty was feeling much, much better. He was excited at the prospect of finding someone else who'd got Miganium and Miganium powers. From time to time Sam took hold of the metallic rock thing and had another go at shifting things with *his* mind, but it didn't work. Ty also checked, every so often, that his power was still intact. It was. And what's more, it seemed to be getting stronger. At one point they came to a deep and very muddy stream which stretched a few metres across. It was just a little too wide to jump and it looked like they'd have to either wade across and risk losing a shoe, or go a long way further down the bank to find a better crossing place. A fallen spruce lay nearby and to his immense surprise, Ty found that he could shift it. With a delighted chuckle at its first hesitant roll, Ty turned, pulled the cool mask of focus down over his mind and lifted one end of the spruce into the air. It pivoted oddly at an angle and Ty could sense Sam staring in disbelief. Then he pulled the end of the log round and dropped it. It fell with a satisfying thud, just reaching the other bank and resting solidly upon it.

With whoops of pleasure and excitement, they ran across it, like small children. 'You are going to be handy to have around!' said Sam, beaming. 'Still reckon you couldn't lift a telly?'

As they walked, Sam told Ty they could get the mail train. It would pass through first thing in the morning, and they could catch it at one of the stations in the north of the county. 'They usually head out between four and five o'clock from main stations,' explained Sam. 'We'll make it to Harcott easily by then. We'll get some sleep at dusk and then set out again about midnight.'

They hiked on and on. Sam was sturdily built for just this kind of terrain and didn't seem to slow down for a moment, but Ty found it harder going. He spent a lot of time at the Croft but he'd only gone on long haul treks with Sam in groups, on a couple of occasions. And then there'd been a long break every couple of hours, as there had been people of all ages and abilities tagging along. So he was exhausted when they finally stopped to camp close to a wide and busy river that wound through the woods.

'Rest,' said Sam, kindly. 'I'll make camp. I know you're not used to this, and you've had one mad day. I also think all that telekinetic stuff you're doing takes it out of you more than you know. You slowed down a lot after the log shifting.'

Ty nodded, too tired to protest, and settled back against a tree trunk to watch Sam do his thing. The ranger shrugged off his backpack and pulled out a small, tightly packed, sausage-shaped bag. He tugged loose its cord and eased a compressed bundle of green ripstop nylon from it. He gave the material a shake and it shuddered and pinged open into a small, pop up shelter, shaped like half a dome with an open front. Sam set it down onto an even patch of ground, after kicking away some large stones, and then set to pegging it into place with hooked steel rods which he emptied from the bag. He then undid a tightly rolled strip of spongy matting which was attached to the bottom of his rucksack frame, bent it back on itself to straighten it and then laid it inside the half-dome tent. Next he gathered armfuls of dry bracken from a nearby glade and tucked it underneath the matting, creating a bouncy mattress.

Ty was amazed when he then pulled *two* lightweight thermal sleeping bags out. He chucked those into the shelter too and said 'Go on—go and lie down.' Gratefully, Ty scrambled into the tent and lay down on the soft interior. Lulled by the comforting noises of roosting birds, babbling water, and Sam pulling more intricate bits of equipment out of his rucksack and preparing the ground for a fire, Ty drifted off to sleep.

Chapter 9

The gentle crackling of the fire awoke him and Ty was surprised to see it was almost dark. Sam was crouching by a small, neat blaze close to their shelter. He had cleared away the leaf litter and built a delicate criss-cross of dry sticks and small branches, which he had taken care to first strip of their bark. Ty smiled to himself. He knew this was a smokeless fire. There was no chance Sam would give away their position, even if someone was looking for them here.

There was a wonderful smell reaching him and as he sat up groggily, he saw that Sam had been fishing in the river. A wild brown trout fillet was stretched through a split stick which Sam had driven into the ground at an angle across the fire, supporting it with another stout forked twig. Hung on a second of these contraptions, on the other side of the fire, was Sam's ancient billy can, which was bubbling and steaming. Another stick was angled in the other direction, with mushrooms snagged along it, beginning to shrink and turn brown. Sam looked around at Ty and beamed. The ranger was completely in his element.

Ty shuffled across on his knees and peered carefully into the can. Stuff was cooking in it. 'What's this?' he asked, curiously.

'Cat tail tubers,' said Sam, comfortably. 'Parasol mushrooms on the kebab stick.'

It was a wonderful meal. As the stars prickled out across the sky between the leaves overhead, they ate fresh hot trout with the nutty mushrooms and tubers. 'I didn't see you carrying a rod,' mumbled Ty, through a mouthful.

'Nah. Don't need one,' said Sam. 'I just use my little hand line wrapped round a can or something. I'll show you some time.'

When they'd eaten they banked the fire down. 'It'll start to smoke if we let it fall to embers,' said Sam. 'But it shouldn't get too cold tonight.' They wandered off into the bushes in different directions for their pre-sleep business, to avoid having to go out again in the night, and then returned to the tent and their sleeping bags. They had plenty of space under the half-dome tent and the dry bracken was still surprisingly spongy after Ty had slept on it. 'OK,' said Sam. 'It's 9.30. We need to be up around midnight to move on and get to the station in time for the mail train.'

'How will we get along in the dark, though?' worried Ty, nestling happily into his sleeping bag. 'Have you got a torch?'

'I have,' said Sam. 'But we won't need it much. There's a full moon up and we'll follow the river. There's an easy path along it. I wouldn't take it by day—there'd be too many people about. But by night it'll be deserted, except perhaps for the odd night fisherman. We'll have to look out for them.'

Ty sank easily back into sleep, his stomach full and warm. The next thing he knew, Sam was nudging his shoulder and telling him to get up. Blearily, Ty crawled out of the sleeping bag and staggered to his feet to help Sam break camp. Everything was tightly rolled and folded and put back into Sam's bag, although Ty offered to carry his sleeping bag in his own backpack. He also changed quickly out of his school clothes and put on the sweat-shirt, jeans and trainers that he'd packed, now very glad that he had. He'd have been a lot easier to spot with his red school jumper on, emblazoned with its emblem and name.

They worked all traces of the dead fire back into the earth and threw the soggy burnt twigs deep into the undergrowth. Sam would have insisted upon this even if they hadn't been fearful of enemies tracking them. A good woodsman never leaves a sign of his presence, he'd often told Ty.

It *was* surprisingly bright as they set out, with a cool white light bathing the ground from the full moon high overhead. Here and there, in the thicker parts of the wood, Sam did use his torch, but after about half an hour they reached the river path that he'd spoken of. It was a glorious walk, with the sights and smells that can only be had in the middle of the night when no other humans are about. Twice they saw a fox run across their path. The first one was gone as soon as they'd laid eyes on it, but the second paused, sniffed the air and then regarded them for some seconds before turning its rump on them and trotting off, its tail straight out behind it.

'It wasn't even afraid of us!' marvelled Ty, and Sam smiled.

'It didn't scent any violence in us,' he said.

At one point they stood still and stared in wonder. Three or four deer and a magnificent stag were standing together in a glade beside the river path, cropping the turf beneath the stars. The antlers of the stag cast an impressive shadow across the silvery grass and Ty and Sam stood, for perhaps two minutes, gazing at the creatures, until the stag suddenly lifted his head and looked directly at them. It turned, with speed, but not with panic, and fled into the trees. The females followed. Ty and Sam moved on.

After an hour along the riverside, they *did* spot a night angler. He was sitting cross-legged on the bank, under a smaller version of Sam's half-dome tent. Beside him was a tin of worms and his rod rested on a prop, the line cast out across the fast running water. From the steam rising above the tent, they guessed he was having a hot drink from his flask. They walked in a wide arc around him, under cover of the trees, and only came back to the river path when they had moved along out of sight.

The pale glow of dawn was beginning to reach across the eastern sky when they arrived at the station. They'd only had to take to the streets for about ten minutes before they found it and were convinced that nobody had seen them. Ty was feeling more and more confident that they weren't being chased in any case, but oddly, as they walked into the orange sodium glare of the station lights, he sensed a movement behind him, and spun around to see what it was. There was nothing there. Nothing at all. 'You've got a touch of the Borages, my son,' he told himself.

By good chance, they had only a few minutes to wait before the elderly mail train clattered in. They were the only people getting on and their carriage was deserted. Sam had bought their tickets to Manchester from the automatic machine on the platform, carefully easing notes into the payment slot and avoiding use of his credit card. Ty made up his mind to repay Sam as soon as he could. Countryside rangers didn't make great money, although you couldn't get a much better job as far as Ty was concerned.

It was just after 4 a.m. and Sam suggested they get into their sleeping bags again and try to doze until the morning brought more people into their train. Ty wrapped himself up in the lightweight cocoon and lay down across the old-fashioned train seat. He loved the rocking and the noises of the train, even it's old, smoky smell—much preferred it to the more modern trains which were taking most routes now—but he couldn't really sleep. Excitement was coursing through him again and all he could manage was a fitful doze. By 5 a.m. the light was streaming into his face, flickering fast like an old cinefilm between the trees and buildings they sped past. Ty sat up. Sam seemed to be asleep, his face squashed into the crook of his arm.

An empty bottle had been rolling back and forth along the floor at the other end of their carriage. The odd rrrrrr-ing noise it made had been one of the reasons Ty had found it so hard to sleep. He couldn't actually see the bottle, but quite instinctively, Ty gave a quick pulse through his mind and the thing rose up immediately, neck first, over the back of the seat near the connecting door. Ty pulled it smoothly through the air towards him, held open his palm and dropped the smooth green glass into it with a musical thud.

'For pity's sake, Ty, you have to stop doing that,' said Sam, quietly. He was in exactly the same position but his eyes were open.

Ty grinned guiltily.

'I mean it,' said Sam, now easing up on one elbow. 'It's getting more and more instinctive in you, which is more and more dangerous. What if you do something when people are here? Someone might already be here for all you know! They might have got in while you were asleep!'

'There's no one here,' said Ty. 'I haven't been asleep.' He placed the bottle meekly on the little shelf by their window.

'And that's another thing. You're going to be tired again soon,' said Sam, sitting up fully now and drawing the sleeping bag around his shoulders. 'You're not used to all the walking and you're full of adrenalin—and if you keep *that* up,' he indicated the bottle disdainfully, 'you're going to exhaust yourself. Promise me you won't do any more, unless you really have to!'

'OK, I promise,' mumbled Ty. He ran his fingers over the Miganium in his pocket and it was warm again. Ty felt a rush of affection for it, but he knew Sam was right.

The first few passengers began to arrive across the next hour, so they stowed their sleeping bags back in their packs and tried to look as dull and uninteresting as possible, hoping not to catch anyone's attention. 'They'll probably put out press reports first, to try to catch up with you,' Sam had said, during their moonlit hike. 'You may well have won us a little time with your story about Devon, but it won't take them more than a day to find out it was a dupe. Then they'll be using the media. So we don't want to get noticed by anyone if we can help it.'

'Surely, though, if we keep sticking to the backwoods, they won't know where to find us,' Ty had replied, earnestly.

'Well, maybe not. But remember, they'll be talking to people who know us and it's not hard to work out where a woodsman would go to hide, is it? They've probably already got other rangers out looking for us, or for signs of our camp. The only thing in our favour is that they have no idea where we're headed—or why.'

At around 7 a.m. they went to the buffet bar and got hot bacon rolls and tea. It was a wonderful breakfast, which they wolfed down, their appetites sharpened by all the walking and the night air. Then they settled back into their seats, not talking much, watching the scenery and trying not to get noticed at every station. Ty *did* sleep a little, after their meal, and when he awoke they were moving through the darker green landscape of northern England. 'We're about an hour from Manchester,' said Sam. He was consulting one of his incredibly detailed lightweight maps, running his finger across the relief lines and emblems of the forests and hills that framed the sprawling yellow and brown markings of the city. 'We'll need to get a city map when we get there.'

Ty felt tremendously excited when at last the train pulled into Manchester. After half a day and a night in the wilderness it was overwhelming; teeming with commuters and traffic and noise. They walked from the platform, sliding their tickets into the exit barriers without stopping to exchange eye contact with anyone. They bought a map book from a kiosk before mooching out towards the buses in a dull and ordinary way. 'Just keep your head down,' said Sam, as they walked past security camera after security camera. He pulled his aged peaked cap low over his eyes.

Outside by the taxi rank, Sam flicked through the map book and found Burnside Avenue, where Bob Parker lived. Instinctively, like water flowing downhill, his finger traced out the quickest route back to woods and greenbelt land. There was a long stretch of wooded gully just behind the street, which broadened into a wide patch of waste ground before following the railway for many kilometres as a skinny copse. This could be a place to head for, if they needed to, he said. But both he and Ty knew they had no idea what would happen today, beyond going to Burnside Avenue. They quickly found a bus which went in the direction of Bob Parker's estate. On board nobody paid them the slightest attention.

Burnside Avenue may once have been defined by a lane of trees, but there was no sign of them now. It was a bleak, concreted street in one of the city's roughest estates. Tower blocks rose, in ugly defiance of any grace, towards the soft summer sky, marking each end of the unlovely road. Between them, cheap, prefabricated houses with wired safety glass in the lower half of their windows lined the dusty pavements, creating a stopping point for drifts of litter which provided the hard grey landscape with a little colour. Children ran about, some in pairs, some in packs, with skateboards and bikes. A group of nine- or ten-year-olds were perched on a tarred black wall, passing around a grubby ready-rolled cigarette. They looked at Sam and Ty with hostile interest as they walked past.

'Hardly Whimsey-on-the-Whey, is it?' muttered Sam, as they scanned the road for something to give them a clue about which house Bob Parker might be in. There was a shop at the base of one of the tower blocks. Its windows were painted out in a dull green colour and there were bars across the door. Inside it was hot and smelled of sour milk from the neglected chiller cabinet. Sam approached a girl on the till, who wore a stained grey tabard and a look of extreme mistrust. 'Do you know where a guy called Bob Parker, lives?' asked Sam, giving her the benefit of his attractive smile.

She looked at him coldly. 'Do I look like a bleedin' oracle?' she said in a thick, Mancunian accent. 'Or did you want to buy something?'

Sam took a deep breath, seized a bar of chocolate from the little tray on the counter and dropped it in front of her. She rang it through the till and held out her hand with a sulky bounce for the cash. Sam dropped the coins in and smiled again. 'About Bob Parker . . . ?' he prompted as she counted it into the till tray.

She rolled her eyes to the ceiling and flicked back her stripy hair. 'He's had enough of you lot,' she muttered.

'What lot? Who do you think we are? We're not press,' said Sam.

'Look—he's up the top end of the road,' she indicated vaguely in one direction, obviously bored with the exchange. A queue was starting to build behind Sam. 'I don't know the number. That's it. *Next!*'

They left the shop and looked in the direction she had waved. It wasn't much help. There were perhaps forty addresses between here and the second tower block. They set off anyway, hoping for something to guide them. Ty noticed a young girl crouching in the gutter in a pink cotton dress and flip-flops. Her hair was in plaits and she wore glasses; she looked about eight. She had a stick and was poking the little bubbles of tarmac that had risen in an oily rash across the road, brought up by the heat. It was a very satisfying thing to do, thought Ty. He'd done it himself, rewarded by the soft popping and puffing of tarry vapour with each prod. He smiled. Then he noticed something. Two boys and a girl, not much older, were creeping up behind the tarmac-poking child with great handfuls of dry grass cuttings, which they'd collected from a sparse yellow verge nearby. They wore looks of pleasure and mean anticipation as they raised great handfuls of the stuff to throw at the girl. There was no wind and they had a direct shot onto her head and the back of her neck as she bent, completely absorbed in her lonely game.

Ty couldn't help it. The minute the grass flew into the air he gave a light pulse and turned it back on its course and batted it straight into the faces of the three children. They squawked in surprise and disgust and began to splutter and cough and rub their eyes. Ty grinned widely and Sam shot him a suspicious look. Ty shrugged and put an innocent look on his face. The girl was looking back over her shoulder in a bemused way. She looked brighter and softer than the others. Ty approached her. 'Good road bubbles, those,' he said. 'I love a good popping session, myself.' She looked up at him, curiously. 'Look,' went on Ty, crouching down next to her at the roadside, 'me and my mate, we really need to find a man called Bob Parker. Do you know which house he's in? Save us from knocking all the doors?'

She squinted up at him. 'Number 56,' she said, pointing her tar-tipped stick towards a house at the far end of the row. 'Two up from us.'

'Thank you. Thanks very much,' said Ty. She shrugged, gave him a brief smile, and went back to her tarmac popping.

The house was well kept, in spite of its setting. It could never be a thing of beauty, built as it was from large pebble-dashed panels around ugly, metal framed windows, freckled with old mildew. But the door had been painted red quite recently and there was a hanging basket outside the front window with some late pansies showing their cheery faces.

They knocked on the door. There was no reply. They knocked again, harder.

'You're wasting your time,' said a voice behind them, and they turned to see a woman with a baby on her hip, eyeing them from the step next door. 'He won't come out. He hasn't been out for days.'

Chapter 10

Sam ushered Ty away from the door, giving the woman a rueful smile and a shrug. The house, being on the end of the row, had a high concrete wall running along the side of it; the barrier between its side passage and back garden and a flagstone pathway that bordered the estate, winding between the houses and the back end of some factory units.

They turned the corner and considered the options. 'Only one thing for it,' said Sam. 'We go over the garden wall.'

Ty looked around him. There was nobody about. He nodded at Sam and the ranger wove his fingers together and stooped with his opened palms ready for Ty to use as a foothold. The swift leg-up sent Ty tilting alarmingly over the top of the wall and he found himself dropping to concrete on the other side in a split second. Sam, fit as he was, hauled himself over just as fast. They stood for a few seconds, listening and watching in the narrow passage beside the house. There was no sound from the garden. It was about seven metres long beyond the back of the house, ending in another concrete wall. In it were some pots with plants and shrubs, grouped together in a pleasant display, and a rotary washing drier with a single white vest pegged to it, motionless in the still air.

They crept down the passage and out into the glare of the yard. They could see nobody through the window into the back room or on the other side of the glass panelled door that opened into the narrow galley kitchen. Just as Ty was trying the door handle a voice boomed out above them.

'Just *what* do you think you are doing in my garden?!'

They jumped guiltily and squinted up into the sunlight. Leaning across the sill of an open bedroom window was a man with white hair, neatly combed back off his clean-shaven face. He was wearing a dark grey shirt and braces and holding a pair of boots. He looked angry, but not remotely frightened. Remembering the newspaper report, Ty could guess why.

'Bob Parker?' asked Sam, in a calm and friendly voice.

'Who wants to know?' replied the man, guardedly, giving them both a steely glare.

'My name's Sam Garner and this is Tyrone Lewis. We really need to talk to you.'

'Look, I told the last bloody reporter who came—
NO COMMENT! Now get off my property before I call
the police.' He went to shut the window.

'*Please!*' Ty cried out, 'We've come such a long
way! It's really important!' Bob Parker snapped the
window shut, but continued to glare at them through
the glass.

'Sorry Sam – but I think this is our only way,' said Ty.
Turning, he focused on one of the many pots. The trail-
ing plant in it shuddered and drooped as the pot rose
smoothly into the air and hovered at head height. Ty
held it there steadily while he turned to exchange a look
with the man behind the glass. Bob Parker was staring
at it, his eyes wide and his mouth beginning to open.
There was recognition in his face. Ty slowly brought
the pot back down, and when he looked up again, Bob
Parker had disappeared. Within moments, though, they
heard the lock being slid across on the back door and
Bob Parker pulled it open. 'You'd better come in, lad,' he
said, with a slight tremor in his voice. 'You too,' he nodded
at Sam.

'A few nights back,' said Bob, settling the tea tray on
the dining table in the back room, 'there was a storm.

Well—in fact, there *wasn't* a storm. Just the beginnings of one, but it didn't rain and it never got here.'

He poured a stream of hot brown tea into each cup, added the milk and some sugar for Sam. 'Digestive?' he offered. They accepted a biscuit gratefully and he settled down onto the chair opposite them, sipping the hot drink. The room was neatly but sparsely furnished, with just the table and chairs and a high-backed armchair in the corner. A clock with a wooden star behind it tick-tocked on the wall as they waited for him to go on.

'When I saw it wasn't going to rain, I went out to water the plants and I found something,' he said at length. 'Something odd, down behind the pots.'

Ty reached into his pocket and drew out the Miganium. He rested it next to the plate of biscuits. 'Like this?' he asked, his heart pounding with excitement. Bob's teacup chattered in its saucer. With a sharp intake of breath, he rested the crockery carefully on the table and reached into his own pocket. Then he opened his palm and Ty saw another, slightly larger chunk of Miganium. He whooped and clapped his hands. 'We knew it! We *knew* it!' he shouted, bouncing up and down in his seat, and Bob began to smile dazedly at them both. He shook his head and let out a relieved sigh. 'I thought it was just me,' he murmured.

Bob insisted he cook them lunch. They hung around in his small, pale blue kitchen while he grilled sausages and boiled potatoes and peas. First he wanted to hear Ty's story, and he nodded and beamed when he heard about the counter-attack on Dom McGill and his posse.

'It's a damn fine thing,' he said with great feeling, 'just to give them something to think about at nights!'

Ty begged him to tell them about the six youths he'd taken on. Bob grinned, clearly beginning to enjoy himself for the first time in some days. 'You should've seen their faces,' he chuckled. 'They just strolled in, calling me granddad and shoving me against the wall. "Come to relieve you of some valuables, granddad!" they went, "Just sit down and be a good old boy and we won't break your legs." I sat down all right. I sat on my front room armchair and watched them going through the sideboard drawers and chucking my stuff about. Then they stepped on a picture of Rose—my late wife—and that's when I just got on with the job. I'd only whizzed a few bits of china around the room before, mind. I was too scared to do all that much when I first found out what I could do. But not any more. I chucked the telly at them first. They didn't know *what* hit them. It's an old one—big and heavy. They thought it was some of the others mucking them about, but the other three had gone upstairs. I've got these swords, too, on the front room wall, ceremonial ones they are, from my army days—and I just slid them up into the air and sharpened them against each other. The lads in the front room—well the two that weren't under the telly—they started screaming at that point. And when the rest of 'em ran down to see what was up, I hauled the fridge out of the kitchen—I don't know how—the plug just came bouncing after it—and sent it right at their nasty faces. Then it was cutlery and plates and the toaster. I didn't let up with the smaller stuff— they could have it as hard as it came.

'By God, it *was* good. I'm not a violent man, but I'm *not* having all that! They ran out into the hallway— except the one under the telly—and then I got them stuck in the corner by the stairs, with the fridge and the toaster and the swords and stuff just keeping them there. I was going to phone the police, but they'd already come. Next door had heard stuff and got them out.

'I dropped all the gear, of course, when the boys in blue got in here. But those lads were scared stiff and wouldn't even move. One of the little toe-rags wet himself. Took me ages to get the smell out of the carpet.' Sam and Ty gaped at Bob in admiration. 'But enough about that,' he said, looking slightly pink. 'Go on, young man. Tell me what happened next to *you*.'

Ty told him about the stuff that Nathaniel Borage had said and how he'd been visited the very next day, as Borage had predicted, by the man and woman in suits. Bob stopped prodding the sausages with a fork and stood up straight to look at Ty. 'Posh woman, old-fashioned hair?' he asked, quickly.

Ty nodded. 'Orange lipstick.' he said and Bob nodded back.

'School inspectors, my backside!' said Bob, shaking the bubbling pan of peas in disgust. 'I know a special operative when I see one. They told *me* they were from the social services—victim support and so on. I could see through them straight away. I did *hope* that I might be wrong, but now I know I wasn't.'

'What did you tell them?' asked Ty, anxiously. He was beginning to feel unsafe in the warm kitchen, despite its fantastic smell of a hot lunch.

'Same as you,' barked the old man. 'Nothing! Said the lads had made all the mess themselves—started fighting each other over who'd get what. Same as I told the police. I may be old but I'm not bloody daft in the head. One word out of place and they'd've had me in the very special old people's home, with no handles on the inside doors. It gets a lot harder to hang onto your freedom when you get over sixty, lad. Nobody under forty thinks you know anything worth hearing and when you talk they tune you out like a radio.'

'So they just went away?' asked Sam, incredulously. 'I mean—they ripped my place apart to find something. Maybe they know about the Miganium. That's what Ty calls it,' he explained as Bob looked at him questioningly. 'But if they *do* know about it, and want to get their hands on it, they're not going to just leave it at that, are they?'

'No,' said Bob, effecting a patient tone. 'No they won't. So what do you think I was doing upstairs when you arrived? Bird watching? I was packing. I'm going up to my sister's place in Newcastle.'

'Bob,' Sam touched the man on the shoulder. 'I don't think you'll be safe even there.'

'Well, you may be right,' Bob drained the hot water off the potatoes and began to mash them. 'Get the plates out will you, lad?' he indicated a cupboard and Ty found three old red-checked plates and laid them on the drainer. 'The point is—Sam, is it? The point is, I don't have anywhere else to go. I've only got my pension now, for what it's worth, and I can only just manage the train fare. As much as I'd like to jet off to Spain, I just haven't got the cash.'

'Come with us,' said Sam, suddenly and emphatically.

'Where to?' asked Bob, but he seemed interested, thought Ty.

'We don't know yet. But if you and Ty have both found this stuff, there must be others. If we can get together, maybe we'll all be safer.'

Bob nodded thoughtfully. 'Let's eat and think on it,' he said. 'Then, whatever happens, we've got to go. They could be back any time.'

The sausages in gravy with mash and peas tasted extremely good, but they had to eat fast. Ty felt very jumpy now. As soon as he'd finished, Bob went upstairs and came down with a holdall. In it were clothes and a thick army blanket. He added some bread and tins of soup from the cupboard, as well as a carton of milk, and a handful of teabags and some sugar cubes in a tub. He hauled a roll of polythene from under the stairs and stashed that inside too.

'Can you manage all that?' asked Sam, doubtfully.

'Young man, I've marched through war zones carrying two thirds my own bodyweight,' announced Bob. 'I think I can manage a bag of bread and trousers.'

Getting out wasn't so easy. They all paused in the hallway, realizing that to troop down the road in full view of the neighbours was not a good idea. 'We'll have to go out the back,' said Sam, eyeing Bob with concern. How

118

would they get him over the wall? He seemed pretty fit for a man of his years, but . . .

'No problem, my young friends,' said Bob, grandly. 'I know a way.'

He led them back out through the garden and into the far corner where a panel in the fence dividing him from his neighbour was loose and tilting at an angle, leaving a gap. Glancing across the neighbour's garden to be sure it was empty; Bob ducked down and squeezed through, dragging his holdall behind him. When they followed, Ty and Sam found that Bob was already half way across the breezeblock wall at the back of his neighbour's garden. It was much lower than his own and on the other side was a stiff bush of fast-growing fir, screening the garden that backed onto it from the other side. Between the hedging and the wall was a narrow space, just wide enough for them all to pass through. They turned back again, skirting the far side of Bob's garden wall and found another broken part of perimeter at the far corner, which rose only to the waist. On the other side was the alleyway. Bob climbed over it easily and they followed.

As they dropped into the alley they heard a noise that made them all jump and stare at each other with dread. A loud rapping was echoing around the corner from the front of the house. 'Mr Parker,' said a woman's voice, which Ty recognized. 'Mr Parker—open up! We're getting very concerned about you.' Frozen, they stared at each other. The woman's voice dropped, but was still clearly audible, bouncing off the hard concrete walls all around them. 'OK, Chambers. Do the lock. We've wasted enough time.' And again her voice rose, with a strident, but oh-so-caring note to it. 'Mr Parker, we've brought an ambulance out. We think you may be ill . . .' These words were so ominous that Ty, Sam and Bob were jolted out of their stupor. They began to run, but then Bob paused, turned back and fixed his gaze on a little opaque window under the eaves at the side of his home. Ty pulled on his arm urgently, but then realized what was happening. Bob wore a look of intense focus. In the still afternoon air, between the murmurs and shouts of the operatives on his doorstep, Ty heard the distinct watery gurgle of a toilet flushing.

'I've just heard him!' muttered Miss Merrill. 'The old goat's messing us about. Get us *in*! We'll see how much messing about he can do in a padded cell.'

Bob turned around again with a grin and they all set off silently down the alleyway, as quickly as they could without creating an echo of their running footfalls. They sprinted through a network of dusty paths until they had covered some distance. Bob was a lot fitter than he looked and only puffed along a little behind Ty. Sam pulled them up to a halt and consulted his detailed map. '*That* way,' he said, with confidence. He was right. After ten minutes of swift walking, they reached the gully that Sam had pinpointed earlier. It was cool and leafy and comforting, if you overlooked the abandoned supermarket trolleys lying in the stream at the bottom, and the odd burnt-out car resting on its tyre-less wheels.

Thankfully, there didn't seem to be anyone else about. 'How far can you walk, Bob?' said Sam.

'As far as you can,' said the old man, stoutly. 'Maybe not as fast,' he admitted. 'Where are we going?'

'We'll head north again. To a more remote area where we can camp. Then we need to get in touch with my friend Nat and see if he's found anyone else. That's as good as our plan gets, right now.'

Bob looked from Ty to Sam, shouldered his holdall and stepped out across the twigs and roots. 'It's good enough for me,' he said.

Chapter 11

Sam was quiet as they trekked across the floor of the gully, to one side of its shallow, oily stream. Ty guessed he was planning their route to a safe camp, so he left him with his thoughts and fell behind a little with Bob, helping him occasionally, over banks or bogs, and asking him more about his Miganium experiences.

'I didn't notice anything for several hours, except that the telly kept fuzzing over,' said Bob. He'd picked up a stout wooden staff along the way and was using it to help himself along, with his holdall thrown over one shoulder. 'It was the next morning that something happened. I was sitting down, looking at the paper, when I realized my reading glasses were across on the mantelpiece. I had my cup of tea and a plate of biscuits balanced just *so*, with the paper on my knee, and I was annoyed that I was going to have to get up again. I sort of squinted at my specs and then they started sliding along the mantelpiece. On their own. I nearly had a heart attack. The tea and biscuits went everywhere.

'Anyway, I was just stuck there in my seat, thinking it was a ghost or something—I even called out to my late wife, in case she'd come back to haunt me! And then I stared at them again and they moved again. And when I held out my hand they flew up in the air and landed in my palm!'

Ty grinned, remembering the shock when his spoon had first started moving about.

'And then I noticed my trouser pocket was warm, and, to be honest, lad, I was so scared I thought maybe it was my bladder giving out! But I stuck my hand in and found the rock stuff and saw that it was all glowing again and getting hot. That's when I made the connection. Since then it's been one very strange week.'

Towards the end of the afternoon, Sam called them to a halt in a holly thicket. 'We're about a mile from a main road, with some shops and a phone, I hope,' he said. 'I need to get off on my own for a bit—and I need you two to keep going on and meet me further up the county.'

Ty started to protest. He was alarmed to think of Sam disappearing, even for a short while. But Sam shook his head. 'I need to get back in touch with Nathaniel Borage,' he said firmly. 'It's the only way we can find the others—if there are any others. Nat promised to keep looking, and I haven't got back in touch with him for more than a day now. He'll be worried—and he may also be able to tell us if there's anything in the papers or on TV or radio about *us* yet.'

'But I need to talk to Aunty Dawn again,' said Ty, 'To keep up the pretence. So we might as well go together!'

Sam shook his head again. 'No.' he said firmly. 'Let me talk to Nat first. If they've found you out, Ty, and they probably have by now, phoning your Aunty Dawn won't be any use, and they'll probably be bugging the line or something. Certainly they'll have convinced her to call them as soon as you make contact. No—you just have to stay under cover. If the public *are* on the lookout for us, they won't be likely to notice just me.'

Sam gave Ty one of his fine maps and pointed out their route north towards the area where he intended them to make camp. They would need to cross two residential roads and walk along the railway for a while, but eventually they would reach a much larger, denser area of wild land. 'Do you remember how to use a compass?' he asked. Ty looked doubtful. He *thought* he did.

'I do,' said Bob, quietly.

Sam nodded, apparently recognizing something in the older man. 'Good. Good man,' he said, clapping Bob on the shoulder. 'Look after each other. I'll meet you at *this* lake.' He indicated a small blue blob on the map. 'Don't hang around in full view when you get there. Just watch it from the trees. I'll go out onto the edge of it somewhere when I'm back, and stay put there until you come to me.'

He gave Ty a reassuring smile and then turned and bounded away through the trees. He moved like a wild animal, thought Ty, like the deer they'd watched the night before.

They both began to tire after Sam had left. The ranger had kept the pace, hauling them along with his high energy and confidence, but now they stumbled a little from time to time and began to trudge, hurrying only when they had to cross the two roads. A car passed them on one of these, and a man in a blue hooded track-suit jogged away from them, paying them no attention. The other, a few minutes further along, was little more than a farm track and quite deserted, although Ty shivered and felt, once again, as if they were being watched.

By the time they'd skirted the railway for half an hour and then trekked further back into the woods, Ty's lack of sleep was beginning to catch up with him. Bob, being several decades older, was also finding the going tough. They stopped for a rest and to eat the bar of chocolate that Sam had bought from the unhelpful shop girl earlier that day, and then pushed themselves on again.

At one point their path seemed almost impossible to move on through. Several young trees had fallen across each other, victims of some recent storm, and neither Ty nor Bob could make out an obvious alternative route. 'We'll have to lift them,' said Ty. They looked at each other and then at the tangle of branches and boughs, and then focused hard. The trees began to tug and bend and pull away from each other, tilting back up towards the sky. But after a few seconds of keeping them upright, Bob and Ty found they could no longer prevent the trees from slumping back together with cracks and woody groans.

Ty could feel the energy sapping out of him and sensed that Bob felt the same. 'Wait a minute,' said Ty, suddenly. 'I've got an idea.' He pulled the Miganium out of his pocket and nodded to Bob to do the same. Then he took the man's leathery hand in his and squeezed it hard. 'Come on,' he said. 'Try to join forces.'

Bob smiled and nodded and said 'Well, lad, it's worth a try.'

They stood straight and faced their barrier, focusing again. This time Ty felt a powerful belt of heat running around his neck and shoulders and spreading through his limbs. He took a deep breath and gave as hard a push as he could. Bob was also focusing hard and the trees shot up high, falling back and away from each other in one fluid movement.

'Yesss!!!' shouted Ty and Bob together. They cheerfully clambered on through their newly cleared path and resumed their trek, comparing notes excitedly on how they'd felt and what they might be able to do next. It didn't last long, however. Only minutes after their triumph both Ty and Bob were doubly exhausted. For Ty, it was as if all his remaining energy had been squeezed out of him like toothpaste. He felt like an empty tube.

'Sam warned me about this,' he muttered to Bob, who was looking grey and old. They were almost delirious with fatigue by the time they reached the lake. At first sight of the water Bob dropped his large holdall and crashed down onto the ground, resting his forearm over his face and breathing shakily. Ty fell down beside him and watched the little squiggles dancing around in front of his eyes again. He felt both terribly hungry and terribly sick and was sweating and shivering, as if he was coming down with flu.

After a few minutes, Bob rolled over onto his side and feebly tugged at something else in his holdall. Then he fell back onto his back with a weary gasp and a small plastic tub in his hand. With some difficulty he pulled the lid off and scrabbled his fingers inside. He pulled out several white sugar cubes and handed them to Ty before digging back in for more for himself. 'Low blood sugar,' he croaked. 'Eat them and you'll feel better.' Ty did so, fighting off the feeling of nausea. Almost as soon as the sugar began to melt across his tongue he sensed some relief. Incredibly, after five minutes and several more cubes, he felt well enough to sit up and look around. So did Bob.

They were under some spruce trees on the thick needle carpet of the wood floor, just set back a little from the lakeside. They retreated slightly into the undergrowth, as Sam had told them to. The lake was small, still and green, apart from the patches of blue sky mirrored in it. It was bordered almost to the water with quite dense coniferous woodland, and only a lightly trodden path around its banks suggested that anybody ever came here at all. There were no car tracks or forestry commission car parks in sight, but one or two more uniform gaps in the trees suggested that the site was visited from time to time.

As the sun began to sink in the sky and midges danced along the edge of the water, Sam returned. He strode into view on the far side of the lake and Ty got to his feet, stepped out from the cover of the trees and waved across to him. Sam nodded and began to hike around to them. None of them shouted out. Not even here. As he drew closer, Ty could see Sam looked pretty tired too, and stressed. He was carrying something which looked like a newspaper, and batted away a few midges with it as he approached. 'Well done,' he said, encouragingly, at the sight of their makeshift camp. Bob had laid out some polythene to rest on and they had begun to collect twigs together for a fire. Bob glanced up at Sam and then handed him the last few sugar lumps from the little tub. Sam took them with a nod of thanks. He sat down on the polythene, crunching, and said, 'The game's up at home, Ty.'

He handed Ty the rolled up newspaper, which he'd folded open at page five. It wasn't a local one, but a national. Ty's eyes widened in disbelief. There, in grainy black and white, was his last school photo. It was a frightful shot. His teacher had insisted that everyone have their hair brushed to within an inch of their lives before they went in to the school photographer and Ty's naturally bouncy dark thatch had been combed through with water, despite his protests. It looked like a dead cat on his head and he was smiling in a tight and extremely sarcastic way and looking just a bit mad. The only good thing about it was that it was pre-brace. His teeth were crooked, but not in a cage.

Next to it was a much better shot of Sam, in his county council ranger uniform. The headline read:

BOY, 13, POSSIBLY ABDUCTED BY RANGER

Ty gasped and shouted out loud. 'No!' He hadn't prepared himself for this. Groaning, with Bob peering over his shoulder, he read on.

A WILTSHIRE schoolboy has disappeared after running away from school to meet his ranger friend in woodland, read the article. It already sounded ominous and utterly, utterly misleading.

Tyrone Lewis, 13, was last seen by his head teacher on the final day of term at Swiftwood Secondary School in Afton Park, Wiltshire, before he cut afternoon classes and vanished.

'We believe that Tyrone went to see a man by the name of Sam Garner, a countryside ranger who had befriended him,' said investigating officer DC Tony Phillips this morning. 'The alarm

was raised by the school that afternoon and the boy's aunt and guardian became alarmed when he did not return that evening.

'Tyrone had apparently called his aunt with a story about visiting a friend in Devon, but has not arrived at his friend's house, and the friend denies all knowledge of arranging a visit.

'We are concerned that Tyrone may have run away from home with Sam Garner, as this man has not been seen by colleagues, or been in contact with his employers, since lunchtime of the same day, although he is believed to have withdrawn a large sum of money from his bank that morning.'

Police say that Garner, 28, who lives at the tied bungalow on Kestrel's Croft where he works, has an unblemished record with the council. It's thought he may have sympathised with the boy, whom he got to know on a series of countryside and wildlife courses, after a number of bullying incidents at school.

'But we can't rule out that Tyrone may have been taken against his will,' said DC Phillips.

Ty groaned again.

**Police are appealing to the public for help
in finding Tyrone, last seen wearing his school
uniform with a red jumper. He is about 5ft 5ins
tall, with slightly wavy dark hair, of skinny build
and currently wearing a brace on his teeth.**

Oh, thanks a bunch! thought Ty.

**Sam Garner is 6ft 2ins with fair hair and an
athletic build.**

The report ended with a crime desk phone number.
Ty handed it back to Sam. 'I'm really sorry,' he said, miserably. 'I think I've lost you your job. At least.'

Sam smiled wanly and patted Ty on the head.
'Can't be helped,' he said. 'I've got more to tell you.
I think Nat's found someone else. I got him on the
phone, although he wouldn't let me say who I was.
He's convinced the authorities are tapping the lines.
Anyway, he started chatting to me, calling me Charlie,
like he was just passing the time. He started going
on about some of the funny stuff he'd been reading
on the internet. Told me that there was this barmy
report of some hairdresser who'd saved the life of a
man when the car he was working on collapsed on

him. Apparently lifted the whole thing off him, single-handed, before the fire and rescue crew got there. Bit of a heroine. She said she'd been taking iron pills or something. There were several witnesses. She didn't say much else. Too modest. Didn't want all the fuss. So I said, wow, how interesting, then he told me about some other nonsense, just to fudge it all up a bit. That's it. What do you reckon?'

Bob and Ty looked at each other. 'Did he say where this hairdresser was?' asked Ty. Sam handed him a scrap of paper, which he'd scrawled on in pencil. It read: 'Tania Mason. Cutting Edge Hair & Beauty' and an address followed. 'It's only about fifteen kilometres further north of here; small town called Camwick,' said Sam.

'So that's where we're going tomorrow, then?' asked Ty and Sam nodded.

'I only hope we're not too late for the lass,' said Bob.

That night they ate the bread and soup that Bob had brought with him, heating it up in Sam's billy can over another smokeless fire, and later carried lake water back in the washed out soup tins to be boiled until it was safe to drink. They made hot tea with Bob's supplies and talked about their plans. Bob, it turned out, had quite good survival skills himself after twenty-five years in the army. He'd joined up at eighteen and seen action in Suez, Borneo and India—where he was injured in a bomb blast and had to be stretchered home.

'Were you badly injured?' asked Ty.

'I can't really remember much about it,' said Bob, draining the dregs of his tea from one of the soup tins. 'I was out cold for quite a while; lost a few days. Took some shrapnel to the head, they say. In fact, they reckon there's still some in there,' he tapped the back of his skull comically and shrugged. 'Never caused me any problems.'

He helped Sam and Ty with the fire and was quite expert in setting up the sleeping arrangements. They put up the half-dome tent again, but it wasn't big enough for all of them. Sam said he'd sleep under the stars, but Bob pulled his trusty roll of thick polythene up between two trees, creating a low shelter overhead. 'Just to keep some of the bugs off you,' he said. 'Or in case it rains.' They bedded down, Sam and Ty in the thermal sleeping bags and Bob wrapped in his warm blankets, sharing the tent with Ty. Sam was perfectly content with just a bed of soft and springy spruce boughs, lending Bob his thermal ground mat. Sometimes Ty thought Sam could have *grown* out of the woody earth.

'Well, Camwick and Tania Mason tomorrow,' murmured Ty, sleepily. 'When do we start out?'

'At dawn, right after breakfast,' replied Sam. 'Hush. Sleep now. You've both overdone it today. Catch up while you can.'

Ty smiled, remembering the joint lifting of the trees, and decided he'd own up to that tomorrow. He dusted a confused ant off the edge of his sleeping mat and fell asleep.

Chapter 12

Both Tyrone and Bob awoke to find Sam already lighting the fire. The dawn chorus was joyous in the middle of the wood and the sun was sending slanting shafts of pale light through the trees. They scrambled out of their sleeping bags to help and Sam sent them off to look for wild mushrooms. 'Try for puffballs or chanterelles or parasols,' Sam called to Ty. 'There are some beech trees off in that direction,' he pointed west. 'About five minutes' walk. You may well find chanterelles there.'

Sam didn't fret about whether Ty would find the right mushrooms. Ty had been on one of his fungi courses and had proved his knowledge of edible mushrooms several times since. Even the chanterelles, which could be confused with another highly toxic variety, he had little difficulty in recognizing. Bob found some puffballs first, their little pale orbs poking out of some conifer stumps, and they harvested a dozen or more with great glee. Moving on to the thicket of beech trees, they did indeed spot some clumps of pretty egg-yolk coloured chanterelles, which Ty turned carefully, checking their gills to be sure they weren't deadly imposters and sniffing them for the faint apricot scent he wanted. They hurried back to camp cheerfully, depositing their goodies next to Sam. A wonderful aroma was drifting around him. He told them he'd picked up some sausages during his jaunt to the shops yesterday. He'd chopped these into chunks and was frying them in his billy can, with a little of the oil that he always carried among his rucksack supplies. He dropped the chanterelles in with them. The puffballs he dusted off and sliced with the sheath knife from his belt before dropping them in to the can too.

They ate with great pleasure, feeling refreshed from sleep and keen to pack up and get moving. With all the metal containers cooled in the lake and stowed away, and the fire put out and carefully covered over, they moved on.

Sam estimated that they'd reach Camwick by late morning. The closer they got, the more people they would encounter. They were heading back into civilization. At the edge of the first road they came to they checked each other over, trying to look as normal and everyday as possible. Ty found it difficult to tell if they looked normal or not. Nothing had been normal for some time now. Bob and Sam both had some stubble in evidence, but this was quite a fashionable look; they wouldn't stand out.

Camwick was a small, pretty market town, which spread along a river. The three travellers wandered through it without speaking much, nervous and watchful but trying hard to look relaxed and inconspicuous. It was market day and there were many people about. Ty felt that odd prickling of hairs on the back of his neck again; the feeling he'd had several times now, that they were being watched. He would have dismissed it, once again, as the Borage Effect, except for one thing. As they crossed the little hump-backed bridge that led down into Wick Street he looked back over his shoulder and noticed a jogger. The man had his head down and hood up, running steadily on the approach to the bridge. Ty couldn't see his face but the blue track suit and its hooded top looked just the same as the one he'd seen on the lonely road through the woods which he and Bob had crossed yesterday afternoon. Ty gulped and wondered whether to say anything to the others, who were walking on ahead of him.

But the jogger turned suddenly, following the river path before he reached the bridge. Ty sighed with relief. He was getting paranoid, that was all.

Cutting Edge was like thousands of other salons across the country, with its bright yellow façade, painted with its name and a pair of scissors, and a large glass window through which they could see several customers wrapped in yellow nylon ponchos, having their hair tended to.

Sam, Ty and Bob sat on a bench conveniently placed on the pavement opposite, wondering which of the staff was Tania Mason. They were all dressed in unflattering yellow tabards, over a selection of high fashion—and there were at least six of them, any one of whom could be Tania.

'There's nothing else for it,' said Sam, pulling a few notes out and handing some to Ty and to Bob. 'We've got to have a trim.'

Bob pulled a face. 'I haven't got enough hair as it is, lad!' he protested, but he got to his feet and followed Ty and Sam across the road.

In the end it was easy. Ty remembered that his mum always asked for the same hairdresser when she went to get her hair done. He thought this was something worth trying. Copying exactly the tone she used, he walked up to the girl at the appointments book and cash register and said cheerily, 'Any chance of a quick trim with Tania?'

'Hang on,' said the girl, who had violently burgundy hair piled into a pineapple shape on her head. She rang her finger down the day's bookings and then called out 'Tan? Have you got time before your 12.30, to give this lad a trim?'

A girl at the far end of the salon checked her watch. She was pretty, with smooth, lightly tanned skin and her hair done in streaks of blonde and light brown. Her brown eyes seemed troubled though; there were shadows underneath them and she looked as though she hadn't slept well. Tania eyed his hair speculatively. 'Wash and a wet cut, love?' she asked. Ty nodded, feeling excitement spread through him. 'Well, I can do you if we're quick,' she said, kindly, and walking over, took his arm and led him to one of the basins at the back.

Sam and Bob looked at each other, then sat down to wait on a squashy yellow leather couch. 'We're with my grandson,' explained Bob, leafing through a magazine.

Ty was wrapped in one of the yellow ponchos and bent backwards over the odd, kidney shaped basin, which dug him hard in the back of the neck while Tania rinsed and lathered his hair swiftly. 'Naturally wavy,' she said, distractedly. 'That's nice . . .'

'No it's not,' said Ty. 'I wish it was straight.'

'Oh, everyone says that,' she replied. 'If it was straight you'd want it wavy.'

Ty doubted that severely but said nothing. He was trying to work out how he'd broach the subject of Miganium and sudden telekinetic powers in a crowded hair salon. She rinsed the shampoo efficiently and then slicked a little conditioner across his head.

'Going anywhere nice for your holidays?' she asked, but Ty could tell she wasn't really listening when he muttered something about Dorset. She had a haunted, faraway look in her eyes when he glanced up. Closer to her, he thought they looked a little pink, as if she'd been crying. She rinsed him again and then abruptly sat him up and folded a towel around his head. She led him to a chair by a mirror, where he gazed at a geeky boy with a towel turban and a brace, deciding that the Dorset holiday might be his way forward.

'They've got great rocks down there,' he said enthusiastically. 'Fossils and that, too. They call it the Jurassic Coast.' She smiled and made a vague expression of interest as she towelled his hair briskly and then began to comb it through. 'That's nice. You into all that rock stuff then?'

'Yeah. I want to be a geologist when I'm older,' improvised Ty. 'Or maybe a palaeontologist. I love dinosaur bones and fossils too. The Dorset coast's covered in them.'

She made another encouraging noise, glancing nervously across at the window and pulling her sharp scissors from a jar of blue anti-nit solution. Expertly she began to snip across his crown and down towards his right ear. 'Short back and sides, is it?' she checked and Ty nodded. In his mirror he could see Sam and Bob, trying not to stare too hard at them. Bob was doing a good job of being absorbed in Woman's Own.

'I've found some really interesting rocks,' he went on conversationally. 'I found an amazing one recently. Have you ever found anything . . . like that?' She paused in her rhythmic snipping and looked at him in the mirror, her smile slightly frozen. 'Like what?' she asked.

'Like—you know—an unusual rock or stone. Something that you'd want to take home and keep,' Ty urged, watching her carefully. She took a sharp breath and then shook her head firmly. 'No. No, I'm not really into all that stuff.' She resumed her fast, efficient snipping and little clumps of wet hair fell onto his yellow shoulder. Ty dug his hand into his pocket and brought the Miganium out, keeping it under his poncho. He waited until she'd finished his right side and had stood back a little and then he pulled the rock out and put it on the small glass shelf in front of them. 'Here's what I found,' he said, quietly, watching her intently in the mirror. Tania froze, her scissors motionless above his head. He saw the colour drain from her sun-bed tanned features and she raised her eyes to his reflected gaze with a look of great fear.

Suddenly she dropped the scissors with a clatter and ran a few feet to the back of the salon, vanishing through the door which had a TOILET sign on it. The neighbouring hairdresser looked up in surprise. Ty shrugged at her, pocketing his Miganium again. 'Said she needed the toilet badly,' he said. 'Actually—so do I. Is there a gents?'

'Through the door, opposite the ladies,' said the girl and Ty darted through immediately, aware that Sam and Bob were getting up and exiting the salon. On the other side of the door, both toilet doors were ajar, the cubicles empty. Further down the little lobby was a small kitchen and a store room filled with shampoo and dyes and other supplies in boxes. A side door led out onto a small paved yard and here Ty found Tania, stripped of her tabard, trying to climb over the brick wall. As Ty approached, she slumped down again, her high heeled boots not suited to the task, and then backed against the bricks, staring at him with dread in her eyes.

'What's the matter?' asked Ty. 'Why are you so scared?'

'I've had *enough!*' said Tania, in a shaky, whispery voice. 'I didn't mean for any of it to happen and now I've had enough!'

'It *was* the Miganium then,' said Ty. 'You found some too, didn't you? And then you floated that car off that bloke. You should be proud! You saved his life!'

'Yeah well, that's fine, but I want it to stop now. I don't like it!' she insisted, desperately, tears welling up in her eyes. 'I can't sleep properly. It's nothing but trouble. You must know that.'

Ty considered this. Certainly his life hadn't gone smoothly since finding the Miganium, but he wouldn't change things now, not for all the world. 'But it could be fantastic,' he said. He pulled a clean tissue from his pocket and floated it over to her in a bizarre but sympathetic gesture. She stared at it, horror-struck. 'You too then?' she whispered.

'Yeah—me and my friend Bob. And Sam's looking after us. Tania—you probably need looking after too. Once this gets out, you get visited.'

'I *know* that!' spat Tania, angrily, still backed up against the wall, her arms tightly folded. 'I've had reporters and accident investigators and people just wanting to say how wonderful I am. I'd never have done it if I'd known.' She paused for a moment, collecting the airborne tissue and scrubbing her nose with it. 'Well, maybe I would have. But I'd have been more careful. I just wasn't thinking. I don't want to keep talking about it. I'm going home.' She turned and started trying to scramble away over the wall again. Ty sighed and dragged a heavy wrought iron garden table across to the wall for her, with his hands and mind in a swift partnership.

'Thanks,' she said, and clambered up onto it. She swung her leg over the worn red brick and dropped down on the other side of the wall with a click of her high heels. 'Oh no,' Ty heard her mutter. 'What do *you* want?' Grinning, Ty took off his yellow poncho and followed her. On the other side of the wall was a pavement leading back down towards the river. Sam and Bob stood on either side of Tania, who had buried her head in her hands.

'Why won't people just leave me alone?' she wailed and when she raised her face to them her mascara had left little black puddles under her eyes.

'Listen lass,' said Bob, kindly, putting his hand on her arm. 'If you're in the same situation as Ty and me, you need help. People will come after you. We came to see if you wanted to join up with us, so we can all be a bit safer and see what we're meant to do with these powers.'

'I'm not meant to do *anything!*' hissed Tania, starting to walk away from them. They hurried after her and she went on. 'I've got a nice, ordinary life. I've got a nice flat and a nice boyf—' she gave a little sob. 'I *had* a nice boyfriend. Until I turned into *Wonder Woman*. Then he dumped me. Said all his mates were laughing at him. I've got a nice job,' she went on shakily. 'I hope. I might have lost that now too. But I've still got my flat and that's where I'm going and you lot can just leave me alone.' She broke into a trot, clipping along the paving stones and up the steps to the hump-backed bridge. They looked at each other and then Sam darted ahead of them, keeping up with her as she began to run determinedly across the bridge.

They could see him trying to reason with her and as they caught up Ty heard him say, 'This is *serious*, Tania. You can't just pretend it's not happening. It *is* happening. And you could be in danger.'

At last she stopped and looked at him. A helplessness washed over her features as if she badly wanted Sam to sort everything out.

'Listen,' said Sam as they joined him. 'Ty and Bob only just managed to get away. The authorities want them and they want the Miganium too. That's your rock stuff. My home was completely wrecked because they were looking for it and Bob was nearly thrown into a padded cell because he wouldn't go quietly. Ty ran away from home and the police are after us both—I've now got a reputation as a child abductor. We're not doing all this for fun.'

She twisted her fingers together and stared at her boots, breathing shakily and clearly trying to work out what to do. 'Come with us.' said Ty. 'Or they'll get you and do tests on you and stuff. If you can lift up a car you must have a pretty strong dose. They'll be scared about national security.' Tania looked at him with a fresh fear dawning. 'But I've got to go *back*,' she said. 'Even if I'm coming with you. I've got to go back home first.'

Sam and Ty and Bob looked at each other. They felt very nervous about Tania going back. 'We can buy you some spare clothes and things,' offered Sam.

'No, you don't understand,' said Tania. 'The rock— that Miganium or whatever you call it—I flushed it down the toilet last night after my boyfriend dumped me.' They gaped at her in horror. 'It's all right though,' she said miserably. 'It's still there. Damn thing wouldn't flush away. Just sits there, looking at me. I had to hold on this morning, until I got to work.' Ty wondered why she hadn't just hooked it out again, but her nails were beautifully manicured and polished so he guessed it was a girl thing.

'Come on,' said Sam, putting his arm around her shivering shoulders. 'We'll go back and get it and grab a few of your things and then get away. Is it far?'

'No—just five minutes' walk,' she said quietly. They followed her in silence until they reached her road. Here, they walked uneasily, keeping a close eye on the people around them.

'Does everything look normal to you?' asked Sam. 'No unfamiliar cars or suspicious looking people about?' Tania shrugged and shook her head. She stopped at a blue painted door and pulled a pair of keys out of the pocket of her black jeans. She let them all in and led them straight up the stairs to her flat. As she went to unlock the door she gave a small cry. It had pushed open without resistance.

'Someone's broken in!' she breathed in a terrified whisper. Sam pulled her back and went in ahead. They followed anxiously. Tania's flat was a mess. Her stuff was strewn across the floor of the main living area; even her framed prints of black and white movie stars were lying, glass cracked, by the skirting board. The drawers in the tiny kitchen and the lilac-painted bedroom were hauled right out and thrown across the floor, their contents scattered all around. Tania gave a sob and dropped to her knees to retrieve the pieces of something pale blue and china.

Whoever had wrecked her home appeared to have left. They stood around, shocked. Then Ty ran into the bathroom and threw up the lid of the toilet. He let out a sigh of relief and a grin spread over his face. Glinting up at him beneath the small well of blueish water, was some more Miganium.

Chapter 13

Ty plunged his hand down the toilet and retrieved the glittering rock, and almost immediately it seemed to warm up against his skin. Stopping only to give it a wash under the tap and dry it with a fluffy peach towel, Ty ran back to Tania triumphantly. 'Top hiding place!' he said. 'They never thought of looking down the toilet!'

She received and pocketed it with much less enthusiasm. She had begun sadly gathering a few things from the mess all around them. Sam was urging her to hurry and Bob was carefully watching the street below from the living room window.

When she finally agreed that she'd got enough stuff—she'd filled a glittery drawstring back pack with spare clothes and cash and a few treasures—Tania swung the thin straps around her shoulders over her black skinny-rib top. She looked a bit like a cat burglar, thought Ty.

'Shoes?' said Sam and she nodded and found some trainers, swapping them for her impractical boots.

As they were about to leave there was a sudden shrill ring, which made them freeze. Instinctively Tania went towards the phone but Sam put his hand out to stop her. She shot him a look of frustration as the answering machine clicked on. 'Hi there!' chirruped a Tania from a much happier time. 'Sorry I'm not at home right now. Leave me a message and I promise I'll call you back as soon as I can. Here comes the beep!' The machine did beep and then they heard a girl's voice.

'Tania? Tania—are you there? It's Clare from the salon. Where are you, love? Listen − if you're there phone us back. There's been someone official in to see you. A man and some woman with a god-awful fifties hair-do and lipstick from hell. They showed us council ID and stuff and they're going to wait over the road for half an hour in case you come back. They were asking about that funny rock stuff you were showing us yesterday. I said you might have gone out for a sandwich or something. I hope you're OK. You've been looking a bit off colour, Tan. Phone me back. I'll try your mobile too.'

'That's them,' whispered Ty as the machine gave a small hum and switched itself off. Almost immediately, another phone went off, with an irritating tinny version of a recent chart hit. Tania pulled a tiny red mobile phone out of her back pocket. She held it in her palm, looking at it as if it was an unexploded bomb. Sam took it from her and put it on the window sill where it continued to bleep its little tune.

'I can't leave my phone behind!' gasped Tania, looking horrified.

'If you take it with you they'll catch up with us in no time,' said Sam, beginning to usher her towards the door. 'Satellite tracking. Dead easy. Sorry.'

They moved quickly down the stairs and took to the streets heading away from the salon, then turned along the river path. There was a pleasure cruiser just ready to leave, only half full of people keen to drift down the green banks of the river, eating ice creams. 'Come on,' said Sam. 'It's off road, and going in the right direction.' They all ran onto it, paying their fare and sinking onto the slatted wooden benches as the skipper pulled away from the bank.

Ty heaved a sigh of relief as the boat moved into the middle of the river and began to chug away downstream. But glancing over his shoulder he felt himself going cold. Standing on the hump-backed bridge as it slowly receded behind them, was a man in a hooded blue track suit. He was leaning on the stony wall and gazing down at the water. Ty couldn't see his face because of the hood, but he shuddered. Daft or not, it was time to share his conspiracy theory.

'Look . . . everyone . . .' he began, awkwardly, but then he noticed that Bob was staring back at the bridge too, wearing a look of similar apprehension. 'What is it? Did you see him too?' he asked, urgently.

Sam and Tania looked confused but Bob nodded slowly. 'Second time today,' he said. 'He was running along the street past the salon earlier. And of course he was on that woodland road yesterday.'

Ty nodded emphatically. 'I saw him too—yesterday and earlier today, when we first came over the bridge. I think he's been following well before that though. Before we got to you.'

'What are you two talking about?' asked Sam in a low voice. He and Tania leaned in towards Bob and Ty as they explained. 'So you think we're being tracked by a jogger, then?' asked Sam, slightly sceptically. 'Isn't it possible that a sports chain has just had a really good offer on that track suit and everybody's got one?!'

Ty opened his mouth to retort, but suddenly felt shivery again. He looked up across their bent heads and saw another low bridge approaching. With a jolt he saw, once again standing right in the centre of it, the man in the hooded track suit. 'Look,' he breathed and they all turned and stared. As they motored beneath the bridge they saw the figure lean right over the low stone wall. They drifted under the arch, staring up at him in horror, and then, as they emerged on the other side and all turned to look back, they saw he had crossed and was watching them still. Nobody could make out his face; it was completely shadowed by the hood. It was the eeriest thing Ty had ever experienced.

As they sat transfixed, staring back at the bridge, the jogger turned and began to run off to their right and along the river path. As the boat cruised on they gradually left him behind. He made no effort to chase, but just ran along at a comfortable pace, until at last they turned a bend and he was out of sight.

'Do you think he's connected with Merrill and Chambers?' asked Ty, at length.

'He could be,' mused Sam. 'But it's an odd way to go about tracking us, if so. He didn't make any attempt to hide himself—apart from his face. And how on earth did he get from one bridge to the other that fast?' They were all silent for a moment. Ty realized he was trembling. Glancing at Bob's freckled, gnarly hands, he saw the old man was too. Sam stood up and walked down the boat, returning shortly with chocolate ice creams for them all.

They accepted them gratefully although Tania looked at hers slightly uneasily. 'I'm supposed to be on a diet,' she said, wincing. They all stared at her and then Sam said 'Make the most of it—you'll probably be eating nettles before the day is out.' It made them all giggle (Tania clearly not realizing that Sam meant this literally), and this helped the tension to evaporate a little.

'Where does this boat go, Tania?' asked Sam, appraising his chocolate flake and biting the end off.

Tania swallowed a mouthful of ice cream without enthusiasm and pointed along the river. 'Just around that bend there's a stopping point, near the bowling green, but we can carry on down to the nature reserve too. We'll be there in about twenty minutes.'

Sam nodded and got out his intricate maps, holding his ice cream well away from them. After some minutes' study, during which Ty anxiously scanned the river and its banks in both directions for the hooded blue figure, Sam nodded firmly. 'The nature reserve,' he said. 'We can get quite deep into woodland there—it links onto a forestry commission enclosure and a reservoir site. The reservoir would be good. It'll be fenced off to the public but we should be able to get in, with your combined efforts. Then it should be quite deserted. Unless we get really unlucky and bump into some maintenance crew.'

The boat chugged into its first stop and a few people alighted, then it moved back into the middle of the river and headed on downstream. There was no sign of the hooded figure. At the nature reserve they got off and stopped at the little kiosk for supplies. Sam bought crisps and some cartons of fruit juice and Ty bought chocolate. Just as he was wandering away from the small building, Ty noticed the radio. It was playing a news jingle and he paused, wondering if he and Sam had made it onto the radio news yet. The first couple of items were nothing unusual—more on that stricken submarine. They'd given the sailors about three days to live. Ty shuddered; poor men. How terrible. Political stuff followed, then an item on the pop star who'd just had a baby, who was talking about giving herself some time to regain her legendary figure. 'I'm going to be kind to myself,' she cooed. 'Now that I've got baby St Tropez, I want at least two weeks when I can eat carbohydrate.' Ty wondered what it was about pop stars that their babies always had to be named after places. Ordinary people didn't do that. He'd never heard of a kid called Swindon.

Sam wandered across to him to find out why he was hanging around the little kiosk. Ty pointed at the radio and they both listened in. There was nothing about Sam and Ty, but then the presenter said something that made them both narrow their eyes with concentration. 'And finally,' he said, allowing a note of amusement into his voice, 'Shoppers in Brentonstoke town centre were amazed today when a local man appeared to levitate a microwave oven over his head. Police were called to deal with a crowd blocking the road when Darren Carter performed the trick, raising the microwave above head height without visible means of support for several seconds. He later said that the whole thing was an elaborate hoax—and was charged for performing in the street without a busker's licence.'

Ty and Sam stared at each other and then abruptly ran across to the others. 'Where's Brentonstoke?' demanded Sam and Tania looked confused. 'I don't know,' she said. 'Should I?'

'It's back down south,' said Bob. 'About fifty miles. We'd need to drive or get a train. Can we hire a car or something?'

Sam considered this for a while. 'Can you drive, either of you?' he asked Bob and Tania. They both nodded. 'We'll need a licence. Which is a problem, because it's a way of tracking us,' he murmured, almost to himself. 'But I think we may have to anyway.'

'I've got my licence with me. What's all this about?' asked Bob, and they told him what they'd heard on the radio. He nodded. 'Sounds like another one,' he agreed. 'I don't know how we're going to find him though. Might try the local paper for more details.'

They found a phone box near the kiosk and Sam made some calls to find the nearest car hire firm. 'We're in luck,' he said, running back to them. 'There's one about fifteen minutes' walk from here. But I think we should get to our camp and lie low tonight, and then come back through here first thing and get down there for about 7.30. They open early.'

'Why can't we go now?' demanded Tania. 'What's the hold up?'

'I just don't fancy us all in a car in rush hour,' said Sam. 'Too slow—too easy to get seen. First thing will be better.'

Tania sighed. 'I hate camping,' she muttered.

The foursome set off into the woodland, initially sharing their path with couples and dog walkers and families with buggies and small children. Then there was only the occasional mountain biker or pair of runners. Finally they seemed to be alone, moving across the far western reaches of the reserve and into some dense coniferous woodland with occasional rutted dirt tracks and piles of logs. As the afternoon wore on it cooled down and clouds rolled in overhead. 'I think we might get wet tonight,' said Ty, eyeing the sky warily.

'We won't,' said Sam. 'We'll build a proper shelter.'

They stopped to eat crisps and drink juice—and for Tania to quickly finish trimming Tyrone's hair with some scissors she carried in a little leather wrap (she insisted she couldn't bear to leave it undone)—before they moved on to the reservoir site. It was, as Sam had predicted, surrounded by a high fence of hostile metal spikes, painted grey and curled about with ivy, set into a bank of grassy earth which rose up around the site. They could smell the water beyond it and see the early evening midges beginning to shimmy in the air above it.

'OK,' said Sam. 'What can you all do to get us in there?' Bob and Ty and Tania smiled at each other (Tania a little nervously) and linked hands. 'Try that bit there,' said Ty and they all focused hard on a bit of metal work. The hot feeling that rushed down from the base of Ty's skull and out in a steady pulse below his chest felt confident and precise—and he could feel similar heat coursing into his hands from the palms of Bob and Tania on either side of him. By the time they'd finished bending three or four spikes out into a neat, accessible V, they all looked flushed; their eyes glittering. Tania suddenly leaped into the air and then hugged Ty and Bob and shoved Sam affectionately on the shoulder. 'That was *good*!' she cried, in amazement. 'That was really *good*! I didn't feel scared that time.'

As they stepped over the bent metal she told them how she'd found the Miganium in the gutter outside her flat. She'd been shocked rigid when later that evening her magazine had flapped up the bed towards her when she'd wished for it.

'I nearly passed out,' she said as they trod along the banks of the mirror-like reservoir, which was deep and dark in the fading light. 'When I stopped feeling sick, I tried it again – and the thing rose up in the air like a bat! I screamed. And it fell on my head. Then Pete, my boyf . . . my *ex*-boyfriend, came in from the bathroom and said was I going nuts. He thought I'd been screaming over one of the stories in the magazine. Like—"Eeeek! Look at her nose job!" —or something.'

Tania said she hadn't tried any more mind lifting. She'd been too scared. But only the next day, on her way to work, she'd seen a mechanic under a car and watched the jack give way and the vehicle collapse on him. 'He was shouting and gasping and I just ran across to him— but before I even got there the car was rising up,' she said. 'I just got to it and made out that I'd lifted it with my hands. I was freaked out, I'm telling you. Everyone was asking me how I'd done it, and this guy was going off in an ambulance, saying I'd saved his life and it was a miracle and all that. Then there was a reporter from the paper coming into the salon and a photographer and all these other people after it went into the papers. It was mad! Any other time I would have *loved* it! Nobody ever pays me any attention usually—not even Pete, really. The last time anyone made a fuss of me was when I fell off Pete's bike and had to go to hospital. But this was so weird. I didn't want to talk about it.'

'When did you work out that it was the Miganium?' asked Ty.

'Quite soon. Because when the magazine started moving I had the stuff on my bedside table and I could see—and sort of *feel*—that it was glowing. And the next day, I took it with me in my bag and after the car thing, it was actually *hot*. I was scared of it. I'm not now, though,' she said. 'It feels a lot better just being able to talk about it.'

They set up camp under some trees a few metres back from the banks of the still, silent reservoir. But instead of unpacking all their usual gear, Sam sent them off to find large twigs and branches. They gathered as many as they could find and Sam cut a few lower boughs off with his small, sharp axe. He then set about building a kind of frame, using five of the largest and heaviest of the branches, tilted together at an angle and strengthened with smaller, horizontally laid branches at about shoulder height. Ty and Bob helped him, tying the knotty bits of wood together at angles with lengths of Sam's coarse, strong string, from one of his many pockets.

They all started leaning the rest of the branches up against it, creating a good sized, woody tepee. Tania was chuckling with delight, her eyes shining—although she did scream when an earwig fell on her shoulder. When the branches and twigs were all resting together in a large cone formation, Sam instructed them to gather leaves and bark and bits of forest floor to drop onto the structure, until it was smothered in a thick coating of woodland matter, except for the triangular door facing towards the reservoir, and the area at the peak of the cone which, Sam explained, was their chimney. This they left uncovered, with space for the fire fumes to drift up through the steeple of branches.

Inside it was cosy, but large enough for them all to get into. Sam picked up some remaining twigs and began to build a fire, after scraping a circle into the leaf litter in the centre and surrounding it with large stones. 'The stones will heat up,' he explained. 'Sandstone,' he said, looking at Ty and lapsing back into teacher mode. 'Won't explode. Don't ever use flint or slate or rocks out of rivers. They can explode. These limestone rocks are good and stable, and, when we have to damp down the fire, before it starts to smoke, the stones will be hot for some time. They'll keep us warm through the night.'

It was getting late now and they all felt exhausted. Sam was ready to go and fish again, but Bob revealed a couple of tins of corned beef from the bottom of his holdall. 'This'll do us tonight, lad,' he said, kindly. 'With Ty's chocolate and a few of the crisps. We'll boil up another brew, eh?' Ty noticed that Sam looked relieved. He realized his ranger friend was looking really tired and quite pale and felt a stab of concern and guilt. How come Bob had noticed this before he had? He was so used to Sam just keeping going, whatever the obstacles, that it had never occurred to him that Sam could need a rest, too.

They ate the corned beef and crisps and chocolate quietly, all of them worn out from the hike and the camp-building. Then they shared out the bedding they had, using Bob's plastic roll and the ground mats to sleep on. The floor was already very spongy underneath them and they didn't need to collect spruce boughs or dead bracken. In any case, they were all so tired that they could've slept on a railway track. Sam doused the fire quickly and the stones did, indeed, go on to radiate heat.

As he drifted into sleep, Ty heard the first pattering of rain over head. A few drops fell inside through the chimney, but, tucked back under the curved slant of the tepee walls, the group did not get wet.

Ty slept well, apart from one moment during the night, when he awoke and saw Sam, sitting up, looking out of the triangular doorway, a dim shadow in the faint light from the cloudy sky. He was making odd, quiet clicking noises and plucking at the pocket of his ranger waistcoat repeatedly. 'Sam?' whispered Ty, uneasily. He wondered if he was still dreaming. Sam didn't respond. He continued his bizarre behaviour. 'Sam!' said Ty again, more urgently. Sam's hands rested in his lap. He gave a deep, deep sigh, and then lay down and pulled one of Bob's blankets over him.

Ty sank back down again. He shook off the weirdness of the moment, too tired to work it out, and fell back into a dreamless sleep.

Chapter 14

The next morning Sam seemed perfectly normal. Ty only vaguely remembered the odd incident during the night. 'Did you sleep all right?' he asked, as they fried more wild mushrooms and fir cone seeds in Sam's billy can over the fire. Tania was only just waking up, making noises like a kitten from the depths of Sam's sleeping bag, as the dawn light filtered softly into the slightly fuggy tepee. Bob had gone off for what he called his 'morning ablutions', disappearing a little way off into the trees.

'Fine. Slept right through,' said Sam. 'How about you?' He gave the billy can, resting directly on the top of the fire, a little shake and it hissed promisingly.

'Well I did wake up once . . .' said Ty, wondering if Sam remembered. He paused but Sam just went on with his cooking. '. . . but I went straight back to sleep again.'

Tania emerged from the sleeping bag, her streaked hair plastered to her face and the last remains of her eye make-up smudged on her nose. 'What time is it?' she groaned. 'I feel like I've slept on a brick.'

Sam grinned. 'It's 5.30,' he said and she winced.

'I've never been awake at an hour with five in it,' she said, thickly, pushing her hair back off her face. 'Apart from tea time.'

When Bob returned they shared fried mushrooms and the last three packets of crisps. Tania eyed her share of mushrooms, laid on a burdock leaf, with suspicion. 'Are you sure these are safe?' she asked Sam.

'Of course they are,' said Ty, hotly. 'Sam's a ranger, you know. And the best woodsman in the country. He knows his wild food. Eat up!'

Tania gave him a stare meant to indicate that *she* was older than *him* and he shouldn't be so cheeky. But she tentatively picked up a fried parasol mushroom with her fingers and put it in her mouth. She raised her eyebrows and nodded. 'Not bad,' she said. 'Not bad at all. But if I start foaming at the mouth later, I'll know who to blame.'

They ate quickly and then packed up their stuff. It was hard, demolishing their beautiful tepee, but Sam wouldn't hear of it being left. Not one track, not one clue of their presence was to remain.

It took them an hour to get back to the nature reserve and they trekked through it without meeting anyone, reaching the road by 7.15. Here, a few cars passed them as they walked quietly through the awakening streets, still slightly damp after the night's rain, and found their way to the car hire building. They had decided that Tania would hire the car. She had her licence in the wallet in her backpack, and Bob realized he had actually left his back in Manchester. 'Anyway,' he said wryly, 'There are probably restrictions on hiring to pensioners.'

Tania went into the hire shop with some more cash from Sam's rapidly depleting roll of notes and emerged several minutes later with a key attached to a large yellow fob. 'It's the Peugeot down there,' she said. 'The green one. Looks quite nice, doesn't it?'

It felt odd to Ty, getting into the neat little car, with its freshly valeted scent, after the sights, sounds and smells of the wild. They all wiped their feet self consciously, first. 'OK,' said Tania, turning the key in the ignition, 'Which way?'

They reached Brentonstoke just as the shops were opening. Its modern, paved precinct was relieved by a few leafy plane trees, planted in a row, with wooden benches beneath them. It was pleasant, if not pretty, and a few early shoppers were already about. Ty caught the wonderful smell of bacon frying and nudged Bob. He pointed longingly to a white van parked under one of the trees, and dug into his pocket to see how much money he had left. Breakfast seemed like a long time ago. They all wanted another one.

The white round bread was fresh, soft and cool, its inside coated liberally with butter and crammed full of thick, dark pink bacon with crispy brown rind. Ty stopped to squeeze a dollop of brown sauce onto his from the large pump dispenser and then they all sat together on one of the benches beneath a plane tree and munched in silence and deep, deep appreciation.

As he finished, Sam beckoned to Ty and they went back to the vendor in the van, who was wiping down the melamine surface of his little hatch and whistling cheerily. Sam bought a couple of bottles of water and then asked the vendor if he knew where they might find Darren Carter—the guy who'd been pretending to float a microwave. The man shrugged and pulled a face under his little stripy cap. 'I've seen him around,' he said. 'But I don't know where he lives. Try *him*, though. He might.' He indicated a mass of rags and hair crouched in a shop doorway some way off. Sam turned and headed for the down-and-out, and Ty followed. Sam dropped onto his haunches and said, 'Excuse me, mate.' The bundle of rags and hair shifted like a small avalanche and the man lifted his face to Sam.

'I'm looking for Darren Carter,' said Sam. 'Bloke at the bacon van reckoned you might know.' The tramp said nothing but looked longingly at the van. Sam paused and motioned Ty back to it. They bought another bacon roll and a styrofoam cup of tea and returned to the down and out. Sam set the cup down by the tramp's feet and handed him the roll.

'Cheers, mate,' said the tramp, accepting it quickly. Ty noticed that his voice was much younger than he looked, and sounded educated. He guessed he would never know why this man was sleeping in doorways. 'You could try the squat down Benson Square,' said the man through a mouthful of bacon. 'I think he lives there.'

'Benson Square,' repeated Sam. 'Do you know what number?' The tramp shook his head, licking bacon grease off the tips of his fingers. 'It's the one that's boarded up,' he said and couldn't tell them any more.

Sam looked at the large scale map of the town centre on a tourist information booth and found Benson Square just a short walk away. The house was in a street full of dilapidated Georgian houses. A huge, sprawling buddleia bush entirely filled its front garden and they had to duck under this to reach the door—or what had been a door. These days it was a large piece of chipboard, which had been nailed into place, but was now pulled off and just tilted back against the frame. Sam pulled the chipboard back and an evil smell of stale wine, smoke and damp wafted out at them. Tania wrinkled her nose and stepped back.

'Hello!' called Sam. 'Anyone there? We're trying to find Darren Carter . . .'

There was a thud and a scuffling noise somewhere in the depths of the house and at length a voice called back. 'He's down the nick. Push off.'

'What—where? Where do you mean?' called back Sam, as they all looked at each other anxiously.

''E got done last night!' called back the voice, impatiently. 'He's down the nick. Now shut the bloody door.'

Sam let the chipboard fall back into place and turned to the others with a shrug. 'I guess we have to find out where the local magistrates' court is. We're probably too late though. Merrill and Chambers have probably got him by now.'

'I saw a sign for a police station near where we parked,' said Ty. 'It could be near there.' They headed back up into the town centre, stopping to check again on the map on the tourist information booth. Ty had guessed right—the magistrates' court was in the same building as the police station. They reached it after a few minutes and walked cautiously up its wide stone steps. There were quite a few people about considering it was a Saturday. The high, vaulted roof arched over two stone staircases to galleries above them and the marble floor was littered, incongruously, with red metal benches with an assortment of people sitting on them waiting to be called into court.

Sam politely stopped a woman, wearing black court robes. 'Is the case against Darren Carter coming up this morning?' he asked, confidently. She eyed him curiously. They were all looking pretty scruffy by now, after three nights sleeping in the woods. 'We're family,' explained Sam. She nodded and consulted a thick concertina of print-out paper.

'Court Three,' she said at length. 'Coming up any minute.'

They ran up the stairs and followed the signs to Court Three's public gallery. Pushing open the thick, heavy panelled doors, they trooped quietly into the hush and reverence of the court room. It was carpeted, wood-panelled and still. From the public gallery, which had only a few students in it, making notes, they could see the clerk of the court, and the magistrate in a dark suit, flanked on either side by two women. Other official look-ing people were dotted about, and a dark haired young woman with a notebook and pen, and another sheaf of print-out paper, sat at the press bench, looking sleepy.

Leaning over the brass railing along the gallery wall, Ty could see a young man standing with his back to them in the dock. His hair was short and clumped and bright pink. Wearing army combat trousers and a thin, crumpled black shirt, he was bobbing up and down on the balls of his feet in a nervy way.

'Mr Carter admits he was drunk and disorderly,' a woman in a black robe was saying to the magistrate. 'He didn't intend to frighten anyone and was in fact, proclaiming the lyrics of a song he'd recently written, rather than trying to incite violence. He admits that his behaviour may have been perceived as threatening, par-ticularly to the members of a Women's Institute gather-ing who were passing at the time. His comment of *"Cheer up, darlin'—you've got a face like a sack of rusty spanners,"* was intended as a joke. He would like to apologise sin-cerely for any distress he caused, particularly when he insisted on displaying his most recent—er – *piercing*—to the lady in question, in an attempt to calm the situation.'

Ty snorted and Sam's shoulders were shaking. The pink-haired man in the dock hung his head, but kept bouncing on the balls of his feet. He seemed to be jingling slightly.

'I fail to see how offering up a septic wound for inspection is in any way comforting,' said the magistrate drily.

'True,' admitted the man's lawyer. 'But Mr Carter was at the stage of drunkenness when many people feel that the world is their friend, your worship. And as I understand it, one or two of the ladies *did* express some interest in his body jewellery, perhaps wanting to help diffuse the situation. Mr Carter tells me that one of them kindly offered a wet wipe and a sticking plaster.'

The magistrate sighed. 'Nevertheless, Mr Carter, this is the second time in as many days that you have stood before me. Yesterday it was for busking without a licence and dangerous balancing of a microwave oven. Today it is wilful lyric-proclaiming and possession of an offensive sore. I'm going to give you one more chance. You'll be fined fifty pounds for being drunk and disorderly in a public place. But, I warn you, if I see you again, I'll be seriously considering a custodial sentence.'

The pink haired man bounced higher on the balls of his feet and jingled louder. He said 'Thanks! Thanks, your honour!' Still bouncing, he was led away by an usher, and Ty spotted the source of all the jingling.

Darren Carter's face was covered in metal piercings, from his eyebrows to his lips. As he hopped down from the dock there was a movement in the seats below and Ty felt his throat constrict with panic. He jabbed Sam with his elbow and pointed urgently. Rising from the seats just below their balcony were Miss Merrill and Mr Chambers. Still dressed in their dark suits, they moved smoothly in behind Darren Carter as he was led out of the court. Bob and Tania peered down at them too, concerned at Sam and Ty's horrified reaction.

'That's *them!*' hissed Ty. 'Quick!' They scrambled up the balcony steps and shoved through the heavy door. Ty and Sam ran ahead and skidded to a halt at the top of the gallery steps, ducking down between the stone balustrades and watching the scene below.

'We're too late,' murmured Ty. Miss Merrill and Mr Chambers had already cornered Darren. They were talking to him animatedly, showing him some kind of ID. He looked curious rather than threatened, and was nodding his head in a vague sort of way. 'They're offering him something,' whispered Sam as Bob and Tania crouched down behind them. Darren was still talking with the suited couple, but then he backed off a little, shaking his head and holding up his hands. He started darting nervous glances around him, as if looking for a way of escape. 'No! No, I didn't. It was all just a lark . . .' His voice, edgy and anxious, drifted up towards them. Miss Merrill purposefully linked her arm into his and began walking him along towards a side exit. Mr Chambers adjusted his tie and fell into step behind them. He nodded at a court security guard who followed them at a discreet distance.

'Look—it was a trick. A hoax,' Darren was protesting weakly as the side exit door swung shut behind him. Ty and Sam and their new friends looked at each other. Then they scrambled to their feet and ran down the stone steps, Bob puffing slightly at the rear. Sam led them out of the front of the building and around to the left. 'There must be a side exit route,' he gasped. 'These buildings always have them, to avoid the press.' They ran around the corner of the court, past the small police station and along a cobbled alley. It was narrow and hemmed with parked cars. Suddenly, Sam hissed at them to get down and they all ducked in between the bumpers of the cars. Ty peered around Sam's shoulder and saw another heavy panelled door swinging open further up the alley. Parked in the middle of the road outside it was a shiny black Mercedes, its engine running and a driver in the seat.

The back door was open and Darren Carter was now being shoved inside, protesting, 'Look—I can't help you, love,' he was saying with a shaky laugh, as Miss Merrill pushed him down in the seat. Mr Chambers stood behind them, scanning the alley. 'Honestly,' went on Darren, his voice now muffled in the interior of the car. 'I can't even wriggle my ears. And I haven't got any of the stuff you're on about. Now, some *other stuff* I can get you . . .'

Ty motioned at Bob and Tania, urgently. They had to do something *now* or it would be too late. 'Tania—you get her handbag,' he hissed at the nervous hairdresser, who squinted at Miss Merrill's unfashionable black bag in disgust. 'Bob—go for his mobile or something,' whispered Ty. 'I'll get the driver out.' He reached back and linked hands with them and they all felt a hot pulse connect them instantly, driven by their high anxiety and the danger they were facing. The scene that followed was very fast. First Miss Merrill gave a gasp and a shriek as her unattractive handbag was suddenly wrenched off her arm and sent high into the air above her.

'Get them away from the car!' instructed Ty and Tania sent the handbag bobbing back along the alleyway just above head height. Miss Merrill shrieked again, looking very panicky, and ran after it. Mr Chambers looked dumbstruck, staring after her, and then started shouting 'Oi! Oi! Oi!' like a deranged market seller as his mobile phone and dark glasses shot up out of his pocket. The phone struck him a nasty blow on the bridge of his nose and then started circling wildly around his head along with the glasses. The man began flapping his hands in the air wildly, trying to grab them back down again. '*Away* from the car!' hissed Ty again and Bob obediently sent the phone and glasses off in the same direction as Miss Merrill, who was now balancing shakily on an empty milk bottle crate, trying to snatch back the bag. Tania grinned menacingly and the bag swatted the woman hard on her thickly-starched hair-do. She fell over into the alley with another shriek and then Tania emptied the contents of the bag on top of her.

Meanwhile, the driver in the car was twisted round in his seat, staring back at his colleagues and shouting. Ty focused his mind hard on the bonnet of the car. He pictured the catch underneath it and slid it hard across and up—and then the bonnet bounced violently up into the air. As he slammed it back down again Ty saw the driver spin back round in his seat and then stare in horror through the windscreen. He let out some ripe language and as the bonnet continued to crash up and down. Mr Chambers and Miss Merrill rolled in the alley, scrabbling for their belongings and trying to avoid the blows from them at the same time, while the driver threw himself out of the car and ran past Sam, Ty, Bob and Tania, hurtling back down the alley and out of sight.

'NOW!' yelled Ty and they all ran for the black Mercedes. Sam shoved Tania into the driver's seat, where she found the keys still in the ignition and the car engine still running.

'Wass goin' on?' cried the pink-haired man in the back, his piercings chinking wildly as his head snapped left and right. Bob and Ty hurled their bags into the footwells and got in on either side of him, and Sam threw himself into the front seat and pulled the door shut just as Tania put her foot down and the tyres shrieked against the cobbles. They shot out of the alley at a dangerous speed and careered sideways into the main road with a screech. Tania glanced in her rear-view mirror, pulled out and then drove swiftly off up the ring road, heading out of town as her travelling companions picked themselves up and fumbled urgently for seat belts.

'Wass goin' on?' cried Darren, again. 'Who are you?' Ty stared back down the road and saw Miss Merrill emerge at a furious run around the corner of the court building. She was actually shaking her fist.

'Have you got one of these?' Ty asked Darren, displaying his chunk of Miganium. Darren stared at it. Bob reached into his pocket and pulled out *his* Miganium. Tania said, 'I've got some too—but I'm driving.'

Darren reached into his shirt and, worryingly, appeared to retrieve *his* Miganium from his armpit.

The rocks glinted and glowed at each other. Ty grinned at Darren. 'Welcome,' he said 'to the Miganium Gang.'

Chapter 15

They left the car in a crowded multi-storey half an hour later, and began to hike away from the town they'd stopped at, towards a canal which led into some woodland, according to Sam's map.

'Couldn't we just keep using it?' Tania had asked, giving the sleek Mercedes a regretful stroke. 'It's a fantastic car.' But Sam had said no. 'It's just a matter of time before it gets tracked down,' he explained. 'I'm amazed that we got this far without getting pulled over.'

But before they left it, they had ransacked the glove compartment and boot for any useful supplies. They'd found a thick blanket, a first-aid kit, several stretchy bungees with tough yellow hooks, an empty canvas sack and a tin of barley sugars. They threw all the booty into the canvas sack and gave it to Darren to carry, as he was the only one without anything on his shoulders. Now, as they reached the banks of the canal and headed fast away from the town, Darren shook his head with a chorus of tiny clinks and said 'So what are you lot then? Some kind of secret society? Who do you work for?'

They all snorted with laughter and Ty began to explain rapidly how they had all come to meet. 'Yeah! Yeah!' butted in Darren when Ty told him about the effects of finding the Miganium. 'I couldn't believe it!' He bobbed and chinked excitedly. 'I found it in a chip wrapper! Can you believe it? A chip wrapper! I thought it might be worth a bit so I kept it, but it was weird, like—it kept getting all warm and sort of mushy— although it didn't actually go soft or anything. But it was weird. I was poking it about back at the squat and then I wanted a beer, right, and this can, right, came right off the window sill and just, like, flew through the air. I screamed. My mate Rab saw it too, but he thought he was trippin' out. So, like, I hands him this rock stuff too and says, '"ave a go, Rab! 'ave a go!" And he tries it too, right, but no—nuffin 'appens. So I have another go and like—whoop—can of beer, right up in my face. I'm telling you, it was like Stephen King! Then Woolly comes in and says what's all the shoutin' about and we get him to have a go, but no—it's only me! Only me! I'm different. I always knew I was different.'

'I'll say,' said Tania, eyeing his clinking face jewellery with disdain. 'I bet you never used surgical spirit on that lot did you?'

Darren ignored her and kept bouncing, swinging his canvas sack across to his other shoulder. 'So anyway—out I go into the yard at the back and there's this old mouldy mattress and I give that a shove. It didn't want to go at first—too heavy. But I squeezes this rock stuff and looks at it really, really hard—you know, like Clint Eastwood in those cowboy films—and it starts to go. I'm like—amazing, man! Amazing!'

'So at what point did you think it would be a good idea to waft a kitchen appliance up in the air in front of a crowd?' asked Bob, dourly. He clearly didn't approve of Darren at all.

Darren's excited grin faded a little. 'Oh yeah. Well, yeah, that was a bit stupid, now I come to think about it. I got a bit carried away. I thought, like, maybe I could give up the singing and guitar stuff, 'cos, like, every busker's doin' *that*. And then I could do magic and really make some money. So I took some stuff down the precinct in a wheelbarrow. It was just a little microwave I found on the tip. But, yeah, it was a bit stupid. People were laughing and staring and really into it when I was doing the little bits, like sticks and bags of crisps and stuff. I reckon they thought it was all wires and stuff. But then I got a bit excited and went and did the microwave, too. And they all started backing off and lookin' scared and that. And then the old bill came in and done me.'

'So how did you explain it?' asked Ty. 'To the police?'

'Well, they never actually saw nuffin,' said Darren. 'They got there when the people started screaming and shouting and I was just trying to get away. So I said I had a mate who was helping me, with wires and stuff, and they just believed that. I've had to keep out of town since, though. Lie low for a bit.'

Tania shot him another look. 'So waving your infected piercings at middle aged ladies is your idea of lying low?' she asked. Darren grinned and lifted up his shirt to examine a metal ring in his naval. It was swollen and red and sticky, and they all made noises of disgust.

'I dunno if it's gonna take . . .' he said, forlornly, digging at it with a grubby finger as he walked along.

Tania slapped his hand away. 'Well of course it won't if you keep poking dirt into it!' she snapped, like an irritated mother. 'When we stop for camp we'll see if there's any antiseptic cream in that first-aid kit. Where on earth did you get it done?'

'In the kitchen,' said Darren.

The canal path led them deeper into woods, but there were still people about. After another twenty minutes Sam led them away from the water as it slid on across the landscape in a high brick aqueduct and they slithered down a steep, woody embankment and along a stretch of tangled undergrowth. Ty had filled Darren in on the rest of their story, with frequent interjections from Bob and Tania. Sam just quietly led them on, from thicket to thicket. When Ty mentioned the mysterious figure in the hooded tracksuit, Darren stopped and went, 'Whoa! Hey—hey! I think I saw that geezer in the crowd yesterday. I thought he was a bit weird because you couldn't, like, see his face and he wasn't getting all shouty and screamy like the rest.'

'What *is* strange,' said Bob, 'is that he hasn't approached any of us. He's been within touching distance more than once, but he hasn't made any approach. Why?'

They all picked their way along in silence for a while, pondering on this. 'The other thing we should be thinking about,' said Bob, 'is why *us*? What is it about we four in particular that we can use Miganium, but nobody else can? What is *different* about us?'

Darren grinned. 'Well, it's pretty obvious what's different about me, old boy.' He flicked his fingers lovingly across the fifteen or so studs, hoops, rings and beads, hanging madly from his features. 'A body total of twenty-one,' he said proudly. 'Fifteen of 'em on me 'ead! I was gonna have some in me teeth too, but it's too hard to do it yourself. You've got to pay a dentist and it costs a pile.'

Ty winced and thought of John Payne putting his brace on him, just a week ago. 'You should be careful what you wish for,' he muttered and Darren peered at his mouth. 'Nah, mate!' He grinned, slapping Ty on the shoulder. 'It looks cool!'

Bob suddenly stopped and looked from Ty to Darren and back again. Sam hacked on through the bushes with his small axe, not looking back. 'Wait up, lad,' called Bob, and the ranger paused and then turned back. Bob was still staring from Ty to Darren.

'What?!' said Ty.

'Metal,' said Bob. 'In your heads. Your brace, Ty, and your—decorations,' he said, with obvious distaste, to Darren.

'So?' said Darren. 'I don't see any studs or braces in your face, old boy!'

Bob shot him a looked of contempt. 'Well, you wouldn't, would you lad?' he said drily. 'My metal isn't worn like a badge. It's *in* my head. Metal casing off a land mine. Been there for the last forty years.' Darren looked awed.

'But what about Tania?' said Ty. 'She hasn't got *any-thing* in her head!'

'Charming!' said Tania, folding her arms. 'Actually, I have got something in my head. When I came off my boyfriend's motorbike that time I broke my jaw. It had to be wired back together and have metal pins put in.' She tapped her pointed chin. 'Still in there.'

Bob nodded, thoughtfully. 'Well—that could be it,' he said. 'Metal in the head—close to the electrical activity in the brain, sort of channelling the power of Miganium into our thoughts.'

Sam frowned. 'But if that's the case, why not me? I've got a load of metal fillings in my teeth at the back. Can't get much closer to the brain than that.'

They pondered this for a while. 'Perhaps,' ventured Bob, 'it's about *pure* metal. The fillings in your teeth will be amalgam—a mix of metals. But I'm pretty sure that the shrapnel in my skull is pure steel. And Ty's brace certainly is.'

'My jaw pins are steel, I think,' said Tania, rubbing her chin.

'And what about you?' Bob asked Darren. 'What's all that stuff made of?'

'Only pure metal, mate,' said Darren, stroking the piercings again. 'Gold, silver, and a bit of titanium. Can't

186

have anything else. I've got very sensitive skin.' Tania snorted. 'It's true!' retorted Darren. 'Base metal brings me out in a rash.'

'So if it's pure metal, maybe all Sam needs is something made of pure metal in his mouth or—or his ear,' said Ty, excitedly. 'And he might be able to do it too!' They looked at each other, wondering. Then Tania started rummaging in her bag. After a while she looked up. 'It's no good. I've left my jewellery bag at home. You could have tried some gold or something. But I've only got the earrings I'm wearing and I don't think you'd fancy that.' Sam grinned. 'Maybe not.'

Then Ty realized he was still wearing his dad's old St Christopher. He undid it quickly. 'Here! Try this! It's silver.' he handed it to Sam, who cupped the chain and pendant in his palm and looked at them all uncertainly.

'Look—we should probably just be moving on, rather than messing around with all this,' he said. Ty suspected he was a little nervous of the Miganium. But everyone said to try it and so Sam, grimacing slightly, dropped the pendant onto his tongue and poured the fine silver chain in after it. He shut his mouth and pulled a face, holding his hand out for Ty's Miganium. Squeezing his fingers around it he turned and focused hard on a small branch on the wood floor a metre or so away. Everyone held

their breath. After nearly a minute of silent anticipation, during which Tania chewed on her lip and Darren
started bobbing and quietly jingling like a Christmas
reindeer, Sam gave a sigh, spat the chain and pendant
out into his hand with a small cough and shook his head
with a rueful grin. He began wiping the St Christopher
on his shirt.

'Sorry, guys,' he said. 'Can't do it. There must be
something else too. Let's get going.'

Disappointed, they started mooching along through
the thicket again, but Sam paused to hand Ty his St
Christopher. As he dropped it back into the boy's palm
his body suddenly stiffened and Ty looked up and
caught his breath, scared. Sam had that same shut down
look that he'd seen last year. Ty tugged gently on his
sleeve. 'Sam? Sam—are you OK?' Sam did not reply. He
did not blink or even seem to breathe. The only movement from him was the ring finger of his right hand,
poised where it had been when he'd given Ty his
St Christopher, which was flicking minutely up and
down, shuddering like the freeze-frame on an old video
recording.

Ty gulped and was just drawing breath to call the
others back when Sam returned. He stepped back from
Ty and blinked rapidly. 'Are you OK?' asked Ty and Sam

looked at him blankly, before suddenly drawing a deep breath.

'Oh,' he said. 'Did I go off?' This time he looked worried.

'Yeah,' said Ty. 'Just for a minute or so.'

Sam turned and they started to move along after the others, who were negotiating a boggy area, skirting some holly bushes. 'Anything else?' asked Sam quietly.

Ty shook his head. 'Only a bit of a twitch in your finger. Do you feel OK?'

'Yes,' said Sam. 'I'm fine. Come on—let's catch up.'

Everyone grew tired fairly quickly following the dramatic start to the day. By lunchtime they were ravenous and Sam led them across some open fields to a river, crossing a couple of quiet lanes. The sun had come out more strongly now, and it was good to feel it on their backs as they plodded across the soft turf, but Ty kept looking around him anxiously as they crossed the lanes. Any moment he expected to see either another black Mercedes or the sinister man in the blue track suit.

They found a small copse of hazel trees close to the river bank, which offered them some kind of screen from anyone who might be looking for them. They made makeshift camp, dropping their bags and sitting on them while Ty shared out the last few chunks of chocolate and

Sam got out his hook and line from a battered tobacco tin and wound it around his empty drinks can. He and Bob went off to the river's edge to fish while Ty, Tania and Darren gathered sticks for a fire. Then Tania and Darren stood back and watched with a degree of respect as Ty piled the sticks in a steep cone, stripping bark off some of them.

'If you take off the bark it doesn't smoke,' he explained, as he laid the sticks in a criss-cross fashion. 'Well—as long as the wood's dry. And you can't let it fall in on itself, or that will start it smoking too.' He had peeled some dry, curly white bark from a birch tree near the river's edge and used this as his tinder, setting it at the base of the sticks. Then he emptied Sam's flint and steel from its worn leather pouch and struck metal against stone, sending tiny red sparks into the tinder. The birch bark took almost immediately and Ty began to quickly feed more curls onto it, placing them on the dry sticks. Soon they could smell and see the sticks beginning to burn with low bright flames—but only a wobbling in the air above the sticks gave away the rising heat.

By the time Sam and Bob returned with two good sized perch the fire was well established. Sam quickly gutted and filleted the fish and then cut a notch in a long green stick to hold the fillets over the fire, as he had done with Ty on their first night in the woods. They shared the fish and ate hungrily. Tania made no noises of concern at the unusual food.

After lunch they talked about what they should do next. 'We can't just keep running for ever,' said Tania. 'And I don't know about you lot, but I'm starting to whiff. I really need a bath. Can't we find a motel or something and just get clean?'

'You could,' said Sam. 'But it's dangerous. I'm not sure where we should be going next. Or what you're all supposed to be doing with the power you've got.'

'Maybe we should form a travelling show!' said Darren, suddenly, with a jingle of enthusiasm. 'We could make a fortu—' He stopped as they all gave him a stony look. 'OK, just a thought,' he mumbled.

'I do think we should be working together a bit more,' said Bob, thoughtfully. 'It would be useful to know what we're each capable of—and what we can do when we link up. It certainly seems to be much stronger when we do that. And it'll help if we need to defend ourselves.' The drone of a light aircraft overhead made him pause and they all squinted up through the trees. Ty guessed they were all thinking the same thing. A spotter plane?

'Probably nothing,' went on Bob. 'But after that little display we all gave in the alleyway this morning, they're not going to give up and go away.'

Sam nodded. 'Maybe we should be thinking about some form of negotiation. Perhaps we should even be thinking about going to the press. There's safety in publicity sometimes.'

They thought about this for a while. Ty wondered what it would be like to live in a world where everyone was fascinated by you and frightened of you in equal measure. It didn't appeal to him. 'I need to find some bushes,' he said, getting to his feet. He wandered away into the denser undergrowth until he could no longer see or hear the others, but only the breeze in the leaves above him and the sporadic drumming of a nearby woodpecker. His business over, he made to turn back but then a flicker of movement in the corner of his eye made him freeze. He turned his head, holding his body as still and quiet as possible, and there it was again—a flash of blue between the trees, maybe fifty metres away. Ty's heart began to pound. The jogger! He was there again!

Ty leaped back over the log he had dropped behind and began to scramble madly back through the wood, tearing the air into his lungs in panic. Cold fear began to pour across his shoulders and down his back as he sensed the jogger closing in on him. Low holly leaves tore at his arms and overhead twigs scratched his face. He didn't even attempt to push them away, but thundered on desperately, feeling the jogger getting closer.

At last he reached the hazel copse and crashed into view of the others. 'Sam! Sam!' he yelled. 'He's back! The jogger's back! He's behind me!' His voice sounded high and scared, like a very young child's. Sam was sitting quite still, looking not at Ty but somewhere off to his right. Tania, next to him, was motionless too, staring in the same direction as Sam, her mouth open. Bob and Darren were also still, their backs to Ty. Confused, scared, and exasperated that nobody was responding, Ty yelled shrilly, 'Everyone! He's right *behind* me!'

'No he's not, Ty,' said Sam quietly and Ty followed the ranger's gaze. Sitting silently on a log a few metres away from the camp, his elbows resting calmly on his knees, was the man in the blue hooded track suit.

Chapter 16

Ty froze. It seemed to him that he stood and stared at the hooded figure for minutes on end, but it was probably only a matter of seconds before Sam reached out and yanked him down onto the ground next to him. Ty saw Sam's right hand fall back onto the hilt of the sheath knife in his belt.

'Stay there. Don't move,' said Sam quietly.

The figure, its head bowed and its face still out of sight, remained sitting for maybe another minute, while they all stared, scared and silent in the quiet wood. Ty could hear Tania's shaky breathing and Darren gulping once or twice, although the frantic thumping of his own heart almost drowned them out.

Finally the stranger spoke. 'You don't need to be afraid, you know,' he said, in an American accent. 'And you won't need that knife, Sam.' The figure raised his hands and slowly pulled the hood off his face and head, revealing a luxuriant coiffure of blond hair and a tanned, clean-shaven face. Tania and Darren gasped and Ty felt his jaw drop. Beaming at them, awash with his familiar oily charisma, was television's own talk show king—Teddy Taylor.

Ty pinched his arm hard to be sure he wasn't asleep and dreaming and Tania gave a shaky scream of amazement. Darren sank forward onto his knees and gaped at the man, who was still beaming benignly around at them all and clasping his hands together as if about to lead them all in prayer. 'Teddy Taylor!' shouted Darren, his voice somewhere between awe and hysteria. 'Teddy Talk Show Taylor! It can't be! You're winding me up!'

Bob and Sam stared at each other, mystified. Neither of them ever watched daytime television and hadn't a clue who the stranger was. Teddy Taylor shrugged in a well-practised, overly-modest fashion.

'I *love* your show, man!' said Darren. 'I couldn't get over Men Who Eat Dog Food in Secret! Totally gross! Brilliant!'

Tania had crept forward too, to get a better look at him. 'Shouldn't you be on, now? Live from Chicago?' she asked, glancing at her watch. Teddy gave a chortle and shrugged. 'They're all recorded. They only go out live in the States, but anyway, I'm not really involved in all that . . .'

'Huh?' said Tania and Darren.

Ty was shaking his head in little brisk movements, trying to clear it. 'Wait a minute!' he shouted. 'Stop! Stop this! This is stupid! What on *earth* would *Teddy Taylor* be doing in a wood in England with *us*? What the heck has this got to do with anything? This is barmy! We haven't even got a studio audience!' he added, then realized how odd this must sound. 'Well . . . have we?' he said, addressing himself to Teddy directly. 'You're not telling me you've been following us around for days just for a quick chat about whether our mums ever tried to sell us for lab experiments or whether our cat is the reincarnation of Elvis!'

Teddy Taylor had the grace to look faintly embarrassed. He smiled at Ty. 'You're right, Ty,' he said. 'I'm not here for that. But actually, I'm not Teddy Taylor either.'

'Would someone please tell me what's going on?' asked Bob, faintly. Nobody tried. They all stared at the man who wasn't Teddy Taylor.

'Do you have anything sweet to eat or drink?' asked the man. Tania fished the tin of barley sugars out of the sack from the Mercedes and held it up, looking puzzled. 'Good,' said the man, still in an exact facsimile of Teddy Taylor's voice, right down to his contrived little chuckle and sigh. 'It may be useful for the shock. Sit down, Ty. Please.'

Confused and disorientated, Ty sat down between Sam and Bob. Tania and Darren sat back too, crossing their legs and gazing at the hooded stranger as if he were about to tell them a story. As it happened, he was.

The stranger took a breath and said 'My real name is,' and there followed a bizarre stream of guttural cackling followed by a high-pitched whine and a hiccup. 'However,' he went on, 'I think you will find that difficult to pronounce, so you can call me Derruff.'

'Derruff,' murmured Tania and Darren, staring at him.

'I'm from a place called Caralleon Eclata—well, something very like that—in a different galaxy to your own. Although this planet is similar, in some ways.' Ty felt the hairs rise on the back of his neck and Bob started huffing as if he was about to protest at all this nonsense.

'I've been here on Earth for about a week,' said Derruff, 'trying to find something that I dropped.'

Ty found himself clutching the Miganium in a panic. Darren had also shot a protective hand into his armpit and Bob was patting his trouser pocket anxiously.

'Yes,' said Derruff. 'That is what I dropped. It was very stupid of me and I apologize for all the disruption it's caused you. It should never have happened.'

'Wait—wait a minute!' protested Darren, raking his fingers through his pink hair in confusion. 'You're telling me Teddy Taylor is from another planet?!' Although this seemed entirely plausible to Ty, Darren couldn't take it in.

'No,' said Derruff, patiently. 'I am not Teddy Taylor. I am Derruff. When I realized that I needed to make contact with you I had to find a form that wouldn't be alarming. I scanned the television channels in your country and discovered a face and body that would be familiar to you all. Also, it seemed that this man was afforded some respect and reverence by his people,' (Ty snorted, remembering Aunty Dawn chanting at the telly in the kitchen), 'and this also seemed to be useful. Of course, I had to keep some degree of disguise when I was among your kind, because they would stop me and ask me to write my name upon pieces of paper. And some would scream and push their mouths on my face.' Derruff wrinkled his well moisturized, tanned brow and added, 'Why would they do this?'

'Search me!' said Ty. All he had ever felt the urge to push on Teddy Taylor's face was a house brick. At speed.

'Well, OK,' said a voice behind him, and Ty saw that Sam was standing up, his hand still resting on the hilt of his knife. 'So you've taken on a human form and you've come to get something back. What? And why us?'

Derruff looked gravely at Sam, turning his head to one side and scrutinizing the ranger. This was quite unlike the talk show host. 'Not you, Sam. Not you. Just your friends. They have the substances that I lost. I need to have them back. Before it's too late. It will be better for you, too.' They glanced uneasily at each other. Not one of them looked willing to hand over their Miganium.

Derruff sighed. 'Let me explain,' he settled comfortably back onto his log. 'Some time ago—around a hundred years back in your time—my planet was hit by what you might know as a meteor. Not a large one, and it didn't cause any damage. At least, not by its impact. The meteor broke into many pieces as it entered our atmosphere and was scattered across the surface of Caralleon Eclata where it was found, over a period of time, by a number of people—200 or more I believe. My people are—*were*—peace loving and civilized, but not perfect. Not perfect at all. The meteor fragments gave them some amazing powers—powers that grew. Powers to shift the seas and control the weather, to bring molten rock out from the bowels of the planet. Powers, in short, which could unbalance and demolish. And that, I'm afraid, is what happened. Now there is no Caralleon Eclata. My planet died within one year of your time.'

They stared at him. Nobody spoke.

'I am here because I was one of a small number of scientists inhabiting one of our moons. Our moons were colonized many decades before and were outposts for research and for watching the universe. We watched Caralleon Eclata die.' Derruff's face now bore no resemblance to Teddy Taylor's in its expression. It was the face of darkest grief. Ty felt his throat constrict at the thought of his own planet dying before his eyes.

'But how come you're here? Now?' he asked.

Derruff looked up at Ty, shaking off his sad memories. 'The meteor that struck our atmosphere only partly broke up,' he explained. 'A large part of it remained in orbit around the planet, but when Caralleon Eclata died, it spun off into space. I tracked its path and realized that it would come into contact with several other inhabited worlds within my lifetime alone. I decided that I must follow it, using my craft and its limited weaponry to shift the meteor's path and keep it clear of contact with other civilizations. It was my duty. To try to make amends for what happened to Caralleon Eclata.'

'Make *amends*?' asked Tania, softly. 'Why make amends?'

Derruff looked at her and to their amazement, tears began to flow silently down his face. 'When the meteor arrived, I was on duty in the observatory,' he said, simply. 'I saw it. But it was so small, I thought it was harmless. I didn't warn anybody.'

There was another long silence as they all took in the awful meaning of Derruff's words. He believed he was responsible for the death of an entire civilization. Of course, he couldn't be. He couldn't have known what the meteor *was*.

'Give it back,' said a firm voice and Sam stepped in among them, holding out his hands. 'Give it back now.' There was a tense silence and then Ty stood up and backed away from his friend.

'No!' said Ty. 'No! Not now! Not yet!'

Sam stared at him. 'Ty! You heard what Derruff said. It's too dangerous. I've always *felt* it was too dangerous. And now I know. You have to give the Miganium back.'

Even Tania and Darren were looking convinced, and Bob was waiting, impassive, watching them all. Ty shook his head again vehemently. 'I'm *not* giving it back yet. You're not going to tell me we've been through all *this* for nothing! You've lost your job and we're all on the government's most wanted list and we've been running around the country like rats through a sewer and there *has* to be a reason for it! There *has* to be!'

Derruff made no move to force Ty to give up the Miganium. He watched, silently as the boy backed further away, but Sam stepped forward, wearing a grim, determined look.

'There's something we have to *do*!' insisted Ty, his heart tearing at the look on Sam's face. He loved Sam like he was his big brother but he would not allow him to take back the Miganium. Ty glanced behind him, ready to run. He didn't know why he felt so strongly now, but he could not *bear* the thought of their adventure ending with such a whimper. He was convinced there was something *else*.

Sam was advancing again, holding up his hands. 'Ty. Come here. Let's talk about this, sensibly.' But Ty recognized the tone of his voice and the control in his movements. He'd seen Sam like this before, just before he'd captured a suffering, fatally injured bird and quickly broken its neck. Ty turned to run, leaping across the log and a patch of nettles and hurtling back through the wood. He heard them all calling him and the steady pounding of Sam's feet behind him. He knew he couldn't outrun the ranger but still he tried, forcing his way into the trees as fast as he was able, the Miganium clutched tightly in his hand. In a matter of seconds he was shoved violently forward onto his belly, smacking hard onto the soft peat and hard claws of roots beneath. His chin hit the slimy edge of a stagnant pool beneath a clump of firs and as the wind was knocked out of him by Sam's ruthless rugby tackle, Ty saw the Miganium fly in up front of his face and land with a wet thud in the middle of the muddy water.

As it sank down out of sight and Sam tried to pull him up by his shoulder, shouting at him, Ty suddenly realized, with perfect clarity, why he had been running; why he had been protecting the Miganium. He flexed his mind with expert precision and the Miganium shot back out of the mud and landed in his palm. Then Ty sprang to his feet and turned to Sam, who was trying to grip his shoulders and keep him from running on again.

'I know *why*, Sam!' he shouted, urgently, gripping the Miganium in a fist of iron. 'I know what we've got to do!'

Sam stared at him, abruptly dropping his hands to his side. His chin jerked violently twice, and his eyes rolled up into his head. Then his shoulders shot back in a sudden and brutal spasm. Ty stared, aghast, as the ranger let out a terrible, rasping cry and then keeled back onto the wood floor. His whole body landed rigid and shuddering and there was saliva on his chin. Only a slit of white showed between his eyelids and there was a blue tinge creeping around his mouth.

'Help!' screamed Ty. 'Oh please! Everyone! Help!'

Chapter 17

They had been running after Ty and Sam anyway and so they arrived only seconds after they heard Ty screaming, finding the boy crouched in desperation next to the fallen ranger, who was now moving like a broken puppet, as if some giant hand held his invisible strings and tugged him viciously for fun.

'Sam! Sam! I'm so sorry!' Ty heard someone crying in desperate, choking sobs. As Tania crouched down next to him and put her arm around his shoulders, he realized the sound was coming from *him*.

Bob and Darren knelt down next to Sam, who was still in the grip of his seizure and looking horribly grey. 'What the hell's wrong with the lad?' asked Bob, and oddly, it was Darren who took charge.

'He's having a seizure—I think he may be epileptic. I wondered why he didn't drive today.' Darren removed the sheath knife from Sam's belt and handed it to Bob. 'Did he hit his head when he fell?' he asked Ty.

Ty shook his head, still convulsed with sobs. 'I—I don't thi-think so,' he gasped. 'He's going to die, isn't he? He's going to d-die and it's m-my fault.'

Tania squeezed him harder and Bob said, 'Of course not, lad.' As he said this, the terrible spasms crashing through Sam suddenly ended and he slumped back into the earth, still. Ty held his breath as Darren leaned over and put his cheek just above Sam's mouth. 'It's OK,' he said. 'He's breathing. It's over.' And then he expertly bent Sam's left leg up at the knee, tucking the foot under the other leg, took hold of Sam's left shoulder and raised knee together and manoeuvred the unconscious man smoothly over into the recovery position.

Then he took off his grubby black shirt, revealing several more piercings, folded it into a small pillow and tucked it under Sam's cheek. Sam's breathing was deepening, as if he were simply asleep. There were pine needles in his hair.

'It was my fault,' said Ty again.

'It wasn't your fault!' argued Tania, still hugging his shoulders. 'How could you have known?'

'I *did* know!' said Ty miserably. 'I knew Sam was epileptic. I saw him have a *petit mal*—an *absence*—last autumn. He told me he'd had them for years, but he hardly ever got them any more. And he thought he'd grown out of the big fits. But he hasn't, has he? Because *I* brought them back!' A large branch nearby rose into the air and angrily threw itself against a tree with a splintering crack.

'But you couldn't have known,' insisted Tania.

Ty shook his head vehemently. 'I *should* have known. I woke up in the night and saw him being really weird in the tepee, just sort of making funny noises and pulling at his pocket over and over again. That's another kind of fit. But I was just stupid and when he stopped I just went back to sleep. I didn't realize what it was but I remember now.'

'I think I saw one of those *absences* you're talking about yesterday,' said Bob. 'While you were out getting the sticks. Sam was getting the fire ready and we were talking and then he just stopped short and stared at me. It didn't last very long. Then he just carried on.'

Ty nodded. 'Yes. That's it. And there was another one this morning. So that's *four* in two days. He's getting worse. And if I hadn't dragged him halfway across the country and given him all this stress he'd probably be fine.'

'It's not your fault, Ty,' said an American voice and they realized that Derruff was with them. The alien who looked like Teddy Taylor stood a few feet away among the trees.

'See?!' said Tania, squeezing him again.

'It's the fault of *all* of you,' said Derruff.

They stared at him in surprise and dismay. Derruff looked grave. 'It is the combined mind power that you're all radiating, brought about by your use of the Miganium, as you call it, which is disrupting the signals in Sam's brain and bringing on the seizures. It was nothing to do with the chase, Ty,' he added, kindly. But they were all gazing at him in horror. *They* were damaging Sam's brain? Instinctively they began to edge away from the unconscious ranger, as if fearful of infecting him.

'His seizures will re-occur, and grow worse,' went on Derruff, 'if you continue to keep and use the Miganium.'

Ty stood and looked levelly at Derruff, his Miganium still tightly clasped in his hand. 'If we keep it, for just one or two days longer, but *don't* use it—except once— will Sam be OK?'

Derruff considered, looking at Ty with curiosity. 'If he continues to be exposed to you all, I don't believe his state will worsen to the point of death for a week or two yet.' It was a frightening statement and they all looked at each other, aghast.

'Ty—we have to just give it back,' said Tania, moving across to Sam and dusting some of the pine needles out of his hair. 'Don't you see? We can't put Sam through this. And anyhow—we heard how dangerous it is. Think of what happened on Derruff's planet.'

'I know, 'said Ty, feeling calmer and more determined still. 'Look—there is one thing I believe we must do. One thing I think we've been *meant* to do, all along. Derruff—sit down with us. We just need a day or two longer and then you can have it all back.'

They carried Sam back to the camp area, where he slept for two hours, during which time they stamped out the fire, covered it over, and prepared to move on. When he awoke he couldn't remember much. The last thing he was aware of was chasing Ty through the wood. They filled him in on what had happened next—and what Derruff had told them.

Sam looked grave and still pale. Ty undid the tight lid of the barley sugar tin and handed it to him. 'So what happens next?' asked Sam, quietly, taking a square orange sweet. 'Are you going to give up the Miganium? If not, I guess we have to part ways.'

'Derruff's going to let us keep it for another day,' said Ty. 'As long as we don't use it between now and— and when we have to.' He told Sam some more of their plans and then they all got to their feet, picking up the bags and backpacks. Darren and Bob helped Sam along, as he was still unsteady on his feet. They offered to carry him, but Sam, still munching barley sugars, shot them such a stony look that nobody mentioned that again. After fifteen minutes Sam shook them off entirely. 'I'm fine now,' he said. 'The sugar's kicking in. I'll be fine.' And he did seem better, building back up to his normal pace across the next half an hour, and hacking through some thick undergrowth with his axe, as if nothing had happened that day.

Ty badly wanted to talk more to Sam on his own. He needed to feel that they were OK, but soon they reached the roads and the suburbs and everyone needed to concentrate on whether they were being watched or followed. It had taken them two hours to reach the railway station, and when they got there they had another hour to wait for the sleeper.

'It's the cross-country, overnight service to Scotland,' said Ty to the others, as they clustered together, digging out what money they had and pooling it together in Bob's cupped hands. 'We'll need quite a lot to get to Aberdeen.'

They counted up their funds. 'It's not enough!' said Ty, dismally. 'That will only cover three of us!'

'And what about Derruff?' asked Tania. 'And where is he, anyway? I haven't seen him since we got to the roads.'

'He said he needed to go on ahead and see to something,' said Ty. 'He'll be meeting us on the train.' Ty realized that Tania, Darren, Bob and even Sam were now looking to him for what they should do next. He felt peculiar. He was so used to following Sam, but Sam, once he had heard of Ty's plan, had handed the reigns firmly over to him. Ty swallowed and tried to think. 'I think we may *have* to use a credit card or something,' he said. 'I know it's risky, but in a few hours it won't matter any more. And this is too important.'

Tania and Bob both offered cards immediately and they went inside to the ticket booth to buy five tickets. When they returned Tania was looking pleased and excited. 'I got us proper cabins,' she said, with great pleasure. 'My treat! Now we can have a wash and sleep on a mattress! Oh joy! I can sort out my hair!' She dragged her fingers through the tangle of brown and fair streaks with a wince.

They bought sandwiches and fruit juice from the station café and found a curved metal bench to wait on. As the hour wore on they all became increasingly edgy. Ty pictured a bright blue laser beam scoring into Tania's credit card and then shooting back through the till, speeding along hundreds of kilometres of telephone wire and directly into a hand-held gadget, clutched in the claw-like palm of Miss Merrill. Miss Merrill's orange lips stretched across her smudged orange teeth in a wide smile of satisfaction and she snapped, 'Chambers! I know where they are!'

Ty shuddered, and shook the thought out of his head. All around them were ordinary people, going about their ordinary business. Reading papers, talking on mobile phones, buying food and drink from the café. Nobody took any notice of the five crumpled looking travellers. Perhaps because they *were* crumpled looking, thought Ty, remembering how he usually avoided looking at beggars and down-and-outs. He anxiously scanned the papers in the stand outside the little platform kiosk. He couldn't see anything else about him and Sam, or about any of them, although the front page story on one made the hairs rise up on the back of his neck. 'DOOMED SUB: ONLY HOURS TO LIVE' it read.

At last the sleeper train arrived, singing along the metals tracks and stopping at the platform with a sigh. Its doors opened automatically and several passengers got off. Ty's gang gathered their bags and trooped aboard in great relief. Tania, clutching their numbered cabin tickets, led the way, looking thrilled. She'd booked three cabins, each with two bunks, taking one for herself. 'Yesss!' She said. 'I can be a girl again!' before disappearing happily behind the navy blue door. Sam and Ty were to share, and Bob and Darren (an odd couple, if ever there was one, thought Ty) went next door.

The cabins were narrow and compact, but well designed with the bunks set one on top of the other into one wall. Opposite was a locker cupboard and a sink set into a small, lit alcove with a mirror above it. There was a further door, next to the locker, which led to a tiny cupboard of a toilet. Ty marvelled at the soft toilet tissue. 'I never thought I'd be so glad to see proper loo roll,' he said, as the train pulled out of the station and began to rock along the tracks, through the late afternoon sun. Taking it in turns, and edging around each other in the small compartment, they washed and brushed their teeth and used the toilet. Ty felt almost human again. Not that he'd minded being a bit wild; he had loved camping with Sam and the others.

They had talked of meeting up further along the train in the dining car, to eat together and plan the following morning carefully, but in the event, when Darren knocked and put his head around the door, they were all of the same mind. 'That bunk and those lovely white sheets just look too good, man,' said Darren, jingling gently and looking rather younger with his pink hair fluffy from being washed over the little sink. He smelled a great deal better too. Tania arrived too at that point, and they all squeezed into Sam and Ty's cabin, with some difficulty, Bob just edging around the door and pushing it shut behind him. Darren looked at Tania and gave a low, appreciative whistle. Tania had changed into some fresh clothes—a white T-shirt and clean blue jeans—and had also washed and towel dried her hair. She'd applied a little make-up too and she looked very pretty, thought Ty. He felt a brotherly affection for her, remembering how kind she'd been to him back in the woods.

'Whoa! Check out the supermodel,' said Darren. Tania shot him a scathing look, but Ty noticed that she was scrutinizing Darren back fairly thoroughly, and didn't seem too put off by what she saw. 'Nice to see you know what shampoo is,' she said. But she smiled after-wards and dropped her eyes.

They all agreed that sleep was what they needed most. Sam, particularly, thought Ty, noticing the dark shadows under his friend's eyes.

'And it's better if we're not seen too much,' added Bob. 'We don't know how long we've got, do we? Before they catch up with us. They might get on board. And where's Derruff?'

'He said not to worry—he'd catch us up. We might not see him until the morning. I think he has his own arrangements,' said Ty. 'I'm sure he'll be back with us in time. I've got a feeling he might be keeping watch for us.'

'We'd better have some kind of code, in case we need to wake each other up in the night,' said Sam. 'Knock twice and then pause—and then knock three times,' he said, demonstrating by rapping on the train window. 'You can do it on the dividing walls too—we'll hear it. I could hear Darren belching, so a knock shouldn't be a problem.

'How'd you know it was *me*?' protested Darren.

'We get breakfast delivered,' said Tania, brightly. 'I asked for it at about seven o'clock—so we've got plenty of time to get ready. We don't get there until about nine, do we?'

'Just before,' said Ty. 'Well done. But everyone make sure that it *is* breakfast and not—not something *else*.' He wasn't quite sure how they could all do this, but sitting now, on the edge of the upper bunk, he was growing more and more tired and longing to sink back into it. So was everybody else. They retreated to their own cabins and Sam and Ty got into bed immediately. Ty pulled down the dark navy blind, clipping it firmly to the sill, and the room was immediately plunged into a comforting gloom.

The rocking motion of the train was relaxing and the noises of the other passengers, still wide awake and bustling around the carriages, began to slip to the edges of Ty's consciousness.

'Sam,' he said, sleepily.

'Mmm,' came the voice from beneath him.

'I'll understand, if you don't want me to hang around with you at the Croft any more, after all this is over.'

There was a pause, during which Ty wondered if Sam had gone to sleep. Then the ranger spoke up in a voice which held a smile, and made Ty feel so much better.

'Don't be so bloody daft. Go to sleep.'

Chapter 18

The sleep was good, if not deep. It was impossible to get to the bottom-most layers of slumber with the train rocking and jolting and stopping and starting at stations.

Whenever the train stopped, Ty was dimly aware, through the soft grey curtain of his drowsiness, that doors were opening and closing along its length, guards were blowing whistles and passengers were talking in muted tones, stowing their luggage aboard with distant thuds. But he was also aware of his steady, slow breathing; could hear Sam's breathing too, and suspected the ranger was more deeply asleep than he. Ty could *feel* the benefit of his relaxed, semi-sleeping state, even though he was being continually roused from it by the action in the train around him. Part of him was also, he knew, on duty like a sentinel, constantly but calmly alert for the arrival of their enemies.

As dawn began to filter gently around the edges of the navy blind, the train travelled for some time without any further stops and Ty did manage to sleep more soundly. He realized this when he was awoken by a knock at the door. It wasn't the code knock, but then a male voice said, 'Breakfast!'

Ty hopped down from his bunk as Sam raised his head blearily from the pillow. Nervously, he eased the door open a crack and saw a man in uniform, holding a tray with a cloth over it. The man looked perfectly normal and unthreatening. He looked about late fifties and his work clothes were worn with use. Ty thought quickly and, before opening the door further, said, 'How long 'til we reach Aberdeen?'

'We get in at 8.48,' said the man without hesitation. 'Barring delays.' He certainly sounded like he'd been saying that for many years. Ty opened the door and collected the tray, thanking him. He drew back into the cabin and shut the door behind him, with a shaky breath. So far, so good. Sam was sitting up now, on the edge of his bunk. Ty sat down next to him and they pulled the cloth off the tray warily. Beneath lay nothing more sinister than two plates with little protective plastic covers on top of them, some cutlery, and a pot of tea and two cups containing punnets of milk and sachets of sugar.

Hungrily, they pulled off the plastic covers and found bacon, sausages, eggs, beans, fried tomatoes and buttered toast piled onto the plates. They groaned with delight and set about their breakfast. Ty would not allow himself to think of the day that lay ahead of them while he ate. He was determined to get a good meal inside him before the butterflies began to rise in his stomach.

They could hear the appreciative noises of Bob and Darren through the wall to one side, as they too received their breakfast. Tania they had heard murmuring her thanks to the breakfast porter and assumed she was enjoying hers in the peace of her own cabin.

Darren and Bob arrived, with the code knock, as Sam and Ty were finishing their tea. Bob leaned around and rapped on Tania's door and she joined them too. Just as they had all managed to settle, with Bob and Sam on the lower bunk, Darren and Ty sitting over their heads in the top bunk and Tania leaning against the cabin window, there was another knock on the cabin door.

They glanced at each other nervously and then heard a muffled American accent. 'It's OK! It's me—Derruff.' Tania let him in and he leaned back in the only space left, against the cabin door. 'Hell—this is one tight cabin!' he said, sounding and looking so like the TV chat show host again, that they grinned at him. Ty half expected him to steeple his hands together and deliver a little pious lecture, about how everyone should respect each other's space or live and let live—in just the way the real Teddy Taylor did at the end of every show.

Fortunately, Derruff did nothing so nauseating. He pulled his familiar blue hood down. 'Are you ready?' he asked them. From their expressions, none of them looked remotely ready, but Ty nodded firmly.

'Yes. We are. I just hope that we've got enough strength between us.'

Derruff regarded Ty for a while. 'There is tremendous strength between you,' he said. 'More than you know. Especially in you, Ty. But you'll have to link up to achieve the power you will need. You'll need to tap into each other in a way that you haven't up until now.'

They looked at him, blankly. 'How do you mean?' asked Darren. 'Do we have to, like, cut palms and mingle blood or something?' He looked both appalled and excited, like a kid who's found a dead animal in the road.

'No,' said Derruff. 'Mingling blood is unnecessary. You all have the same type in any case – apart from Sam, obviously.' None of this was obvious at all. They looked at each other and then Bob said, 'Well, blow me down! I didn't think of that! I'm AB Negative! That's as rare as it gets. Nearly killed me during the war when I needed a transfusion after that land mine. They couldn't get any for two days.'

'I'm AB Neg too,' said Tania. 'I give blood,' she added, proudly. 'And I found out when I got my jaw broken.'

'Whoa! Cool!' said Darren, bouncing up and down on the bunk and making Sam duck away from his feet. 'I'm AB Neg *too!* My dad was, so he got me checked out when I was a kid. You're supposed to tell people in an emergency.'

Everybody looked at Ty. He shrugged. 'I don't know,' he said. 'I may be. I've never asked. My mum's just O Positive I think. My dad might've been AB Negative though.'

'He was,' said Derruff. 'And so are you. It's the thing that connects you all, along with the pure metal near your brains.'

'So we were right about that!' said Bob, clapping his hands. 'Well, blow me down,' he said, again.

'But what did you mean?' asked Sam. 'About the tapping into each other.' He looked worried. Knowing how the Miganium was affecting him, Ty could understand his concerns.

'When you link hands, physically, you will need to try to link mentally and emotionally too,' said Derruff, sounding like one of the New Age gurus that Aunty

Dawn loved to watch on TV. 'If you can channel all your emotional, mental—and *spiritual* —energies around among you, the power of the Miganium will be doubled. That may be enough.'

'*May* be?!' said Ty. 'It *has* to be! We can't fail! We can't!'

'You will have help,' said Derruff. 'I will have more Miganium for you when the time comes.'

'You've got some more?!' asked Tania. 'Have you got a whole pile of it up in your spacecraft or something?'

'No,' said Derruff. 'I can't carry it with me in the craft. It's too destructive. I use the technology I have aboard to store it close to me in a magnetic field for a while and then I eject it in as safe a direction through space as I can calculate.'

'So where is this other Miganium?' asked Ty.

'It's here. On Earth.' said Derruff. 'It's the last bit, and we're getting closer to it all the time. When we collect it, there will be enough power for your purpose. But only if you can tap in to each other as I have explained.'

'We can do that,' said Tania, optimistically. Darren, Bob and Ty glanced at each other, less convinced. 'Why don't we practise?' said Tania, brightly, taking hold of Ty's hand and leaning down to pick up Bob's too. Ty linked up with Darren and Darren reached down to Bob, until they were all connected.

'Wait a bit, though,' said Ty, anxiously, as Sam retreated into the bunk beneath him and stretched out on his back. 'I don't want us to do anything that might harm Sam.'

'Hold up a minute,' said Derruff and dug into the marsupial style pocket on the front of his jogging top. From it he pulled some necklaces. They all blinked in surprise as he held them up in his palms. There were three ropes of glinting, rough cut stones of pink and purple and translucent white. 'You need to put these on, Sam,' said Derruff.

'You must be joking!' said Sam, sitting back up and squinting at the jewellery.

'I'm not,' said Derruff. 'These will protect you to some extent from the effects of the Miganium. They are quartz, rose quartz and amethyst. I was amazed to find them so readily available on your planet.'

'Where did you get them?' asked Ty, amused.

'At the Pretty Things Corner in Dundee city centre,' said Derruff with a completely straight face, and then looked bemused when everyone fell about laughing. 'Why is this funny?' he asked, perplexed.

'How did you pay?' gasped Ty, picturing the scene.

'I did not need to,' said Derruff.

'You mean you *stole* them?' asked Tania, shocked.

'No. I simply agreed with the young woman in Pretty Things Corner that I *was* Teddy Taylor. She screamed at me and pushed her mouth on my face. Why do your people do this?' he asked again.

They all shrieked with laughter a second time and Derruff simply looked more confused. 'You are very strange,' he said. 'I imagine this was some form of homage to the god, Teddy Taylor. And when I had written my name for her on a piece of paper, she said I could take the crystals. Without payment. When I left, she and her colleagues were chanting my name and waving their arms.'

'Blimey,' Ty wiped tears away from his eyes. 'You did pick a winner with Teddy Taylor. And for the record, he's no god. Although *he* probably thinks he is.'

Tania leaned towards Derruff, scrutinizing him. 'What do you *really* look like, Derruff?' she asked.

Derruff regarded her seriously. 'Trust me. You really *don't* want to know.' He leaned across to the bunk and firmly handed the necklaces to Sam who took them with a very unconvinced expression. 'Put them on, Sam. They will help,' urged Derruff and Sam, with a shake of his head, began to undo the little golden clasps. He put two of them around his neck, pulling the collar of his shirt up high to hide them. Then he wound the third, which was elasticated, around his left wrist.'

Derruff nodded. 'When the time comes, take that one off your wrist and put it around the crown of your head,' he instructed, and Sam nodded.

'Shall we try it then?' said Tania, picking up Ty and Bob's hands again. Darren connected with them too and they looked at each other hesitantly.

'What now?' said Ty. Derruff just folded his arms and leaned against the door, watching them impassively.

Tania took a deep breath and let it out very slowly. 'I went to a workshop once,' she said. 'First you have to relax, with deep breathing. Follow me. In . . .' she took another deep breath and closed her eyes. Ty did the same, feeling faintly ridiculous, holding hands with Tania and Darren. Darren was bobbing up and down a little, clearly feeling a little squirmish himself. '*DO* cut out the jingling, Darren,' said Tania, testily, opening her eyes.

'Sorry,' said Darren and stilled himself. They tried again, and this time they made some headway. As the train clattered on over points and hissed along the rails, they breathed deeply and rhythmically and Ty felt something like the peace he had experienced during the night, when he was only just asleep.

'Now,' said Tania, softly. 'You need to think about a really lovely, beautiful, safe place. Imagine you are there, lying down and completely relaxed.' Ty pictured himself lying on the ground at Kestrel's Croft, in a sun-warmed clearing, empty of any people and drenched in the scent of summer grass. Bees were droning gently and the birds were tweeting happily in the trees. A distant light aircraft hummed through the blue sky, leaving a shaky white vapour trail. There was a loud trumpeting noise. Everyone opened their eyes and looked about in slightly dazed disgust. Darren was looking sheepish, 'Sorry. Just got a little bit too relaxed. You know . . . gotta let nature do its natural thing and all that.'

'This is hopeless,' snapped Tania, pinging up the blind violently and opening the window for fresh air.

'What is this gas?' asked Derruff, mildly.

'Honestly, Darren! You're about to commit a feat of . . . of . . . major—wonder!' struggled Tania, pink in the face. 'I would think you'd take it a bit more seriously.' Sam was shaking with laughter, silently in the bottom bunk.

Darren looked shame-faced. 'Look, I said I'm sorry. What was that course about, anyway?'

Tania pursed her lips. 'It was for women who want to take back control,' she said, slightly loftily. 'Women who want to learn to say, Stop! Respect my space! Should've got you and your bowels in for a session—that would've helped us!'

'Hey—what's the time?' asked Ty, suddenly, looking out of the open window and noticing that the train was slowing.

'Half past eight,' said Sam.

'Well, it looks like we're coming into Aberdeen,' said Ty, anxiously, noting the tall buildings and the smell of a major city port. 'We must be early.' For some reason a deep, deep unease was settling into his heart. Sam and Bob were trying to squeeze past him to look out of the window too.

As the train slowed further and the end of the long grey platform approached, Ty knew something was wrong. It took him a few seconds to register what it was. Abruptly, he realized that the platform was completely empty of passengers. True, it was a Sunday morning, but this was a major city station and it was as deserted as a remote whistle stop.

'The train must have speeded up to get here earlier. Why?' murmured Ty. 'I don't like this.' He was aware of Derruff opening the door and letting himself out. As the train coasted to a halt the doors did not open automatically. There was a buzz over their heads and then a tinny voice emitted from the train tannoy system.

'Ladies and gentlemen, we are at Aberdeen station. This is Aberdeen. However, we have been informed by the emergency services that there is a major security alert at the station and at present, nobody is to leave the train. Repeat—do *not* leave the train. We hope you will not be detained for very long and we are assured there is no need for panic. Please remain calm and wait on board until advised otherwise. Ahem. May we remind you that the buffet car is still open for a wide selection of drinks and snacks?'

All along the train, people were hauling down windows and peering outside, calling out, 'What's going on?' and, 'Is it a bomb scare?'

The party of five, cramped inside one cabin, stood looking at each other fearfully. Ty peered out of the window again. The platform was still deserted. The only movement came from the digital numbers ticking over on the beat of every second on the station clock and information board.

Just as he was about to bring his head back in and pull down the blind, Ty saw a bright flash by the main entrance to the platform. A man clad completely in a white suit and a full-face mask had stepped into view. He was carrying a rifle and had a small metal pack on his back, with a breathing line linking it to his mask. Behind him followed four others in identical kit. They looked like soldiers in a nuclear disaster zone and, on closer inspection, Ty saw they were also carrying robust meters like the one Nathaniel Borage had carried, housed in bright yellow metal cages. The white-suited men ran along the side of the train, watching the meters closely, rather than peering in at the windows. There were shrieks of panic from other passengers, but Ty, Sam and Bob just pulled back silently from the window as the men passed, their Geiger counters clicking gently but with no ferocity, just as Borage's had.

When they'd travelled the length of the train and back the men regrouped at the main entrance and gestured to someone out of sight. One or two of them removed their masks and headgear.

And then two figures in ordinary navy suits walked out onto the platform and eyed the train speculatively. Mr Chambers was clicking his pen again and Miss Merrill wore a wide, nasty, orange smile of anticipation.

Chapter 19

Their first thought was to run. They gathered their bags and ran as fast as the narrow corridors and the other, panicky passengers would allow, to the far end of the train. They had thought that maybe they could open a door on the other side of carriage and drop down onto the rails, scurrying across to the opposite platform, unseen.

But the doors would not open. They were automatic, controlled by the driver, and the *locked* button was resolutely red. Nothing would move the door out of its electronic paralysis and none of the windows slid open enough for them to climb through. Using their Miganium power now was not an option—not with Sam so close by—and even if they had been able to get out it would have done them no good. On the opposite platform, more men in white were gathering, armed and scanning from window to window. Back on their platform side, the same thing was happening. Maybe twenty white soldiers had now fanned out along the broad concrete path, covering the entire length of the train. As Ty peered quickly out of the open gap above a door, he saw Miss Merrill and Mr Chambers boarding the train at the far end.

There was a hum on the tannoy above them again and the same voice, sounding somewhat stressed, resumed its communication. 'We apologize for any inconvenience while the national security services mount a search of this train.' There were more screams from passengers. 'We are informed that there is a small group of dangerous activists on board—three men, one boy and a woman. If you see such a group, or any individual behaving suspiciously, please do not approach them.' Ty thought it would be hard *not* to find several dozen people behaving suspiciously *now.* A woman in the next carriage had her head stuck in the narrow window and was screaming in a foreign language, and a man further down was pressed into a corner, chewing on his briefcase like a deranged gerbil.

'Please return to your seats or cabins at once—there is no reason to be alarmed.' insisted the voice, although its owner sounded extremely alarmed.

They stared at each other, grouped in a little lobby between the carriages. 'What are we going to do?'

whispered Tania, looking white and terrified. Darren put his arm around her, but looked no better himself.

'We'll have to use the Miganium—get the door open,' said Bob.

'No!' said Ty. 'We promised Derruff—only *once* more. And we promised Sam!'

Sam shrugged. 'Seems like game over to me,' he said, and grinned wryly. 'Maybe you *should* use it. I've got my Pretty Corner necklaces on, remember.' They could hear menacing footfalls moving down the train and Ty thought he caught Miss Merrill's strident instructions, getting closer.

'Where's Derruff?!' asked Darren. 'He should be here—he should be helping us!'

'He said he was going to get us the last bit of Miganium, remember?' said Ty, sounding calmer than he felt. His heart was beating so fast he was feeling light-headed. 'I expect he's gone to do that.'

'Much good it's going to do us now,' grumbled Bob. 'I think we should use Miganium while we can—get that door open and make a run for it.'

'No!' said Ty, again. 'We won't get more than a metre! Let me think!'

But he didn't have time to think. With a crash of army boots and a chorus of rifle safety catches being released, Miss Merrill, Mr Chambers and at least six white-suited soldiers stepped into view. Miss Merrill stopped dead when she saw them all. Her fingers tightened on the handles of her ugly black bag and a malevolent smile spread across her face.

'Well!' she said brightly. 'Here you all are.'

They stared at her in silence. Sam eased his shoulder in front of Ty, trying to position himself between the boy and the guns. But Ty stepped back around him and moved closer to Miss Merrill. He felt that his desperate heart might fail at any moment but he struggled to control the trembling that shook his frame and to keep his voice steady.

'Yes. Here we are. And you know what we're capable of, so back off.'

He was pleased with his own composure and it certainly seemed to have some effect. One or two of the soldiers glanced at each other uneasily and Mr Chambers stopped clicking his stressed pen and slid it back into his suit pocket.

'We know what you want,' went on Ty. 'And we may be prepared to come quietly and give it to you—but that depends.'

'Depends . . . ?' echoed Miss Merrill, arching one eyebrow. 'Upon what, young man?'

'There is something that we must do. Now. If you help us do it, we'll let you have all the Miganium—and you can test us and do whatever it is you need to do. But first, we need your help.'

Miss Merrill raised her other eyebrow and then folded her arms, still clutching her bag handles tightly.

'Tyrone—you have led me on a merry dance across the entire country. I've had to visit your shoddy school, deal with your dozy aunt, rip apart a bungalow stuffed with dead spiders,' she shuddered, 'I've had to trek through woods and over bogs, spend hours hanging round with the pond life on Manchester's worst estate, break into a nasty cheap house to find a phantom toilet incessantly flushing itself, I've spent a *very* dull morning in a magistrates' court and then had my personal effects sent into a localized tornado around my head *and* my car stolen and my driver reduced to a gibbering buffoon. Trust me—I'm *not* in the mood for any more games.'

She flicked her head sideways and quickly ordered, 'Get the ranger. He has no powers. NOW.'

In a swift and terrible movement, three soldiers had shot across the narrow lobby and seized Sam, before anyone could react. Ty shouted 'No!' but they already had him pinned against the opposite door, a rifle shoved hard up under his chin and digging into the soft skin of his throat. The crystal necklaces glinted bizarrely beneath the weapon.

Miss Merrill was smiling nastily again. 'So then. One point to me I think, Ty. Now, any one of you *could* attempt to use your powers on me or my colleagues— but, let me warn you, my soldiers are extremely well trained and they *will* have shot and killed your friend one second after anything untoward occurs.'

At this point the connecting door to the left of Miss Merrill opened and Derruff walked through. Ty caught his breath in horror—would the soldiers fire?! But they didn't and Miss Merrill, too, seemed totally relaxed as Derruff stopped and pulled down his hood. He went to stand next to Ty, who stared at him in confusion. 'Hello, Mr Taylor,' said Miss Merrill, conversationally, as if they'd just met over the dairy counter at the local shop. Derruff looked at Sam and then at the woman with the orange mouth. He said nothing, but rested one hand on Ty's shoulder.

'Perhaps you should tell your little friend why you're here?' said Miss Merrill in a syrupy voice. 'Or would you be embarrassed if I gave you your reward money now, in front of everybody?'

Everyone gasped and Tania said 'No!' faintly, some- where behind him. Ty turned to stare at Derruff. He looked totally calm and wouldn't take his hand off Ty's shoulder, although the boy was trying to shrug him off in disgust.

'It's true, Ty,' he said, with all that TV charm oozing out of him, 'I did give you and your friends away. I contacted Miss Merrill and Mr Chambers last night while you were all on the train, and told them you'd be getting off here at Aberdeen.'

'But why?!' gasped Ty. 'You betrayed us all! Why?!' Fury was beginning to pound through him and he flexed his fingers instinctively around the Miganium in his pocket. It was warm and getting warmer.

'Because we need them,' said Derruff, simply. 'And we can't go on without them.'

'You're on their side!' stormed Ty, pushing Derruff hard in the chest and staggering back from him. Bob grabbed Ty's arm. 'Steady lad!' he urged. 'Remember they've got Sam.' Ty looked across at his friend, still pinned to the window on the end of a rifle and felt his knees begin to give way. He slumped back against the wall and Bob held onto him tightly, dragging him up.

But Derruff was still calm. 'No, Ty. I'm not on their side. Even *they* are not on their side, but they don't understand it. There is something I need to do. Please move back with your friends and do *not* attempt to move or look round my shoulder. Do you understand?'

Miss Merrill was getting impatient. 'Can we please leave out the psycho-babble? You're not on camera now, Mr Taylor!' Ty gaped. She clearly believed he *was* Teddy Taylor.

Derruff turned and faced Miss Merrill squarely. 'You have a case. I need to have it now. The soldier in the next carriage guards it. Tell him to bring it.'

Miss Merrill put her hands on her hips, her handbag still swinging on one wrist, and stared at him.

'Mr Taylor,' she said. 'You *have* been very useful to us. But I think you overestimate your value. The case stays with my guard and he stays in the next carriage.'

Derruff was unruffled. He put his hood back up. 'I am not Teddy Taylor,' he said mildly. Miss Merrill shot him a sarcastic look. 'Big deal. You're a cheap look-alike. Go on then,' she sighed wearily, effecting interest. 'Who *are* you?!'

'This is who I am,' said Derruff. 'Close your eyes, Sam.'

And then the screaming started.

It began almost instantly, and at first, amid the noise and the strange smell and the wavy lines in the air, Ty couldn't make out *who* was screaming. He knew it was none of his party, which had contracted into a tense bundle behind him, holding onto each other tightly.

237

Sam, too, was screwing his eyes shut and pressing silently back against the window, even though the rifle was no longer pressing into his throat.

Ty began to realize that several people were screaming, but by far the loudest and most wrenchingly awful scream came from Miss Merrill. She had dropped her bag and both her hands clawed in terror at her own face, dragging little ribbons of orange lipstick down her chin. Her eyes were wild and round and bulging and her mouth was stretched in a perfect O of horror, emitting a banshee shriek unlike anything Ty had ever heard. Behind her the soldiers were pressing back against the wall. Two had dropped their rifles and were bashing desperately into the door to the next carriage, trying to get back through it but only getting stuck together. Mr Chambers was frozen to the spot, staring at Derruff. There were tears running down his smoothly-shaven cheeks.

All Ty should see was the back of Derruff's hood, but he knew something truly terrifying was looking out of it. He had no desire to see what it was. And then the smell—the odd, faintly chemical smell—receded, and the wavy lines in the air faded away, and Derruff's shoulders relaxed. Miss Merrill went on screaming, although Mr Chambers was showing some relief and wiping away his tears. Clearly Derruff had put his real face away again.

The soldiers had slumped into a terrified group as one scream went on and on. Mr Chambers turned and slapped Miss Merrill hard in the face and she dropped to her knees and began to rock and keen like a madwoman. Mr Chambers rubbed his palms together. 'I've been wanting to do that for such a long time,' he commented in a trembling voice. He rubbed more tears off his face briskly and gulped twice before taking a breath and raising his eyes to Derruff's face.

'Right,' he said. 'It was the case you wanted, yes?'

Derruff nodded and Mr Chambers strode into the group of quivering soldiers and roughly pulled them out of the way. They fell over as if they were made of plasticine. Mr Chambers strode out into the corridor and they heard him say, in a muffled voice, 'It's OK, madam. Everything's fine now. Everything's taken care of. Please go back into your cabin. You'll be allowed to leave very shortly.'

He re-emerged from the corridor seconds later, carrying a small, brushed steel case. He knelt in front of Derruff, ignoring the dazed soldiers and Miss Merrill, who was still whimpering on the floor, and twisted the lock on the little case before opening it. He stood up and moved back, watching Derruff nervously. In the case was a large glowing lump—about the size of a tennis ball—of Miganium.

'Is there anything else you need, sir?' asked Mr Chambers.

'Yes,' said Derruff. 'Anything the boy wants.'

Chapter 20

Ty had never been in a helicopter before. He thought that his first go was a pretty impressive one. All five of them, accompanied by Derruff and Mr Chambers, were aboard a Royal Navy Chinook. The noise was incredible and, as it lifted into the air, all they could do, strapped firmly into their seats, was stare at each other in amazement and excitement.

David Chambers ('Call me Dave,' he'd said, but nobody had yet) was on board, wearing a lightweight helmet with radio communication gear in it. He was in urgent discussion with the pilot and with a crew on board something he called *The Cormorant*. As they flew out low across the North Sea it gleamed up at them smoothly. The day was fair and mild and only the passage of the twin-rotored helicopter above the water was causing crests of white to rise up. Ty looked carefully at the faces of all his companions. Tania was pale but her eyes glittered with excitement. She was holding Darren's hand tightly and gazing out of the salt-washed perspex window. Bob was smiling to himself, as if remembering something. It occurred to Ty that perhaps only Bob, a war veteran, had been in a similar situation before. Derruff was also looking out across the sea, his face impassive and a faraway look in his eyes. He kept his hands tucked into the pouch on the front of his running top and his hood was still up.

Sam looked remarkably calm for a man who had been held at gunpoint less than an hour before. He still had on his pink, white and purple crystals and was playing abstractedly with the elasticated one on his wrist. He raised his eyes to Ty and gave him a warm, slightly sad smile. *I hope you can really do this*, he was thinking. Ty could tell.

Once David Chambers had recovered himself he'd turned out to be remarkably efficient. After a series of curt phone calls from his mobile, he'd had the stupefied soldiers stretchered off the train in minutes, the white troops recalled to their vehicles and Miss Merrill led away by men in fluorescent jackets who took her handbag from her and said 'It's all right love. It's all right. We'll find you a nice quiet room.' Miss Merrill kept twitching and barking 'Puddle! Puddle!' Fortunately, she hadn't left one.

Then they had all been led off the train, as the other passengers were released in a cacophony of frightened questions and mobile phone calls, and taken to the café, which David Chambers had had cordoned off for government use. From here he'd commandeered a vehicle which shot them across to the nearby harbour in minutes, once Ty had explained what they intended to do. The Aberdeen traffic had been stopped for them. Aboard a Royal Navy frigate was the Chinook, both rotors already a blur in readiness for them all. They were taken speedily aboard, hauled up onto the craft and strapped into their seats before they'd even had time to talk about exactly *how* they were going to do it.

And now that he thought about it, Ty really had no idea how. He leaned forward in his seat and tapped David Chambers on the shoulder. The agent turned around. 'I need to *see* it!' shouted Ty, above the pounding of the rotors above them.

'What?!' shouted back David Chambers.

'I need to *see* a picture of it. We all do—and—and any diagrams or information you've got so we can get our minds fixed on it.' He knew that it was possible to move something out of sight—Bob had flushed the toilet from behind the garden wall, and he had picked up a bottle on the first train journey without laying eyes on it. They just needed to be absolutely confident of exactly what it *was* they were moving—where it was and what obstacles lay in their way.

David Chambers reached forward and consulted the co-pilot. The co-pilot handed him a folder with a sheaf of papers inside, which he passed back to Ty. Some were clearly government documents, some printed off from the internet and some were newspaper articles with glossy graphics, revelling in the 'DOOM' and 'GRIM END' that awaited fifty-nine men on board Her Majesty's Submarine *Castleforth*.

Ty scanned the notes, pictures and diagrams and passed the sheets around for everyone to look at, even Sam.

'We're here,' shouted David Chambers and they all looked down to see a square kilometre of North Sea peppered with ships, boats and even small power craft. There were also two other helicopters in the air, one clearly emblazoned with the red logo of a television station.

As they circled and dropped closer to the waves, Ty saw that they were about to land on what looked like *half* a ship. A huge, red hull lay in the water, perfectly steady and about 400 metres away from the bridge, which floated, estranged from its other half, also perfectly steady in the sea. Ty's eyes bulged and David Chambers laughed near his ear. 'It's a semi-submersible!' he shouted with a grin as they all peered down in fascination. *The American Cormorant.* The middle bit is under water. It's designed to scoop up stricken vessels and then rise up above the waves again. Clever, eh?'

The Chinook made for the hull where a landing platform had been prepared, hovering low across the sea and over the ducked heads of some photographers in a hired trawler, and touched down with a slight bump seconds later. They all unstrapped themselves and Ty jumped out first, helped by a man in an orange boiler suit, who was waiting for them with ear defenders on. Ty's legs felt unsteady and his stomach was churning. What if they couldn't do it after all? No. He shook his head and took a deep breath. They *had* to do it. There was no question of it. Darren, Bob, Sam and Tania were jumping to the deck behind him, Tania's hair flying wildly in all directions.

They ducked down and ran away from the Chinook as it took off again, David Chambers and Derruff close behind them. As the beating of the rotors receded in the cool morning air, they looked around them in wonder. The man in the orange boiler suit headed off towards a hatch at the far side of the deck, saluting as a dark haired man in Royal Navy uniform emerged from it and walked quickly across to them. The orange suited man disappeared below as David Chambers moved to meet the naval officer and they exchanged information in a tense, rapid discussion.

'This is Lieutenant Craig Thompson,' said David Chambers. The dark haired man looked at them with a faint hint of scepticism and nodded curtly. 'He's here to assist you. He's been fully informed.'

The lieutenant walked briskly to the guard rail on the edge of the ship and talked them through the scene below. As well as the semi-submersible there were other craft grouped nearby. Lifeboats and a small grey frigate and a torpedo shaped thing which looked like a floating missile, about twenty metres in length, lay close to *The American Cormorant.* 'That's one of our DSRVs,' said Lieutenant Thompson, pointing across to it. 'Deep Submergence Rescue Vehicle. We've had three of them working around the clock to get to the men.'

'Why isn't it working? Why can't you just winch them up?' asked Tania, desperately trying to get her hair back under control.

The submarine is 120 metres below the surface. It's too deep to just haul it up with ropes and chains. Besides, it's wedged against a ledge of rock.'

'Doesn't it have, like, an escape pod?' asked Darren, leaning on the rail and peering down into the blue-green water.

'It does,' said Lieutenant Thompson. 'But it's not working. We haven't been able to find out why. The forward escape hatch is jammed against the rock and the rear hatch is obstructed by the way the sub is listing. Our divers managed to drill though the stern but found it sealed off and flooded.'

'Is anybody still alive, after all this time?' asked Bob. 'What about radiation and all that?'

'This isn't a nuclear sub, although there may be *some* radiation from equipment on board,' said the lieutenant. 'Certainly not enough to kill everyone within a week. And as far as we know there is still air in the control room, where most of the men are. We've heard tapping from inside the hull—some in Morse code. It seems that most of them are alive – but they haven't got much more air. I think they'll all be dead by lunchtime,' he added gravely. 'Unless *you* can do something about it.' He didn't look convinced. 'We have cleared the area of all rescue personnel for the next fifteen minutes. Fifteen minutes is all we can give you, to . . . do what you do.'

They looked at each other and Ty realized that the time had come. There was no reason to wait, and every reason to go *now*.

Derruff was carrying the case with the final chunk of Miganium. He handed it to Ty almost ceremonially, and Ty put it onto the deck, kneeling to unlock it and extract the glowing substance and roll it back into his palm.

It was much heavier than his own Miganium. Someone had handed it in to a geology professor in Southampton, which is how the government had picked it up, David Chambers had told them earlier. They had only confirmed the connection between it and the strange occurrences around Ty and the rest of his party after grilling Darren's squat mates and the staff at Tania's salon, who'd seen the rock.

Everybody, as if on cue, took out their own piece. The five glinting chunks of strangeness from another part of the universe seemed to know they were in company. They glowed more brightly, shifting in matching colours from green to red to blue to violet, and Ty could feel the warmth emanating from them.

'If we all hold hands,' said Ty, his voice a little croaky with nerves, 'We can clasp all the Miganium in between them. Will that help?' he asked Derruff, who nodded from under his hood. In the corner of his eye, Ty saw Sam move away from the group, sliding the stretchy chain of crystals off his wrist and tugging it down around his head.

'Now—do you all have a picture of what the sub looks like—and where it is? In your mind?' asked Ty. They all nodded at him. Every one of them looked scared. A sea breeze buffeted against them and snatched Ty's words away so they sounded clipped and strange.

'OK,' said Ty. 'Ready?' They nodded, but Ty knew they were bluffing. How could you ever be ready? 'Close eyes then,' he said, taking a deep breath. 'And focus— bring it UP!'

The Miganium pulsed hot in their hands and Ty felt a definite surge of energy. After maybe twenty seconds there was a bubbling noise in the water off to the port side of *The American Cormorant* where the sub had gone down. With a shout, the lieutenant and David Chambers ran towards the guard rail and leaned across it in fasci- nation. Derruff stayed where he was, close to Sam, who had taken the precaution of sitting down on the deck.

Ty realized that, of course, he'd opened his eyes and so had everyone else. 'Stop looking! Keep going!' shouted Ty anxiously, and they all screwed up their eyes again and squeezed their interlocked fingers hard around the Miganium. The bubbling noise ebbed away. They remained, motionless, focusing hard and feeling more and more desperate. Nothing else happened. Noth- ing at all.

After two minutes Ty opened his eyes. Tania was staring at him, tears on her face. Darren was looking at his scruffy boots and Bob was grimacing, shaking his head. 'It's no good, lad,' he said wearily. 'It's too heavy and too far down.'

'No!' Ty's shout was blunted by the wind but his face was sharp and angry. 'We *won't* give up! Derruff! You have to help us! You have to link up with us or something.'

Derruff stepped towards them but he, too, was shaking his head. 'I'm sorry. I can't,' he said. 'Miganium doesn't work like that for me—and it's as dangerous to me as it is to Sam.'

'But you must be able to do something!' pleaded Ty. 'We're not strong enough without you!'

'You are,' said Derruff, 'You're just not motivated enough.' And then he did an extraordinary thing. He turned on his heel, strode towards Sam and then scooped the surprised ranger up in one arm, dragging him to the edge of the deck. Ty blinked in amazement at the strength in the alien's frame as he lifted Sam by the base of his skull and dangled him out over the edge of the sea. Sam had struggled and yelled as Derruff had dragged him along the deck but now that he was suspended above the long drop into the dark sea, snagged in the iron fist of their unpredictable ally, he went suddenly limp. Something seemed to shutter down over his eyes and Ty, staring in horror, realized that he'd gone into another seizure. He screamed at Derruff to stop and started to run towards him but Bob caught a hold of his collar and held him back.

'Wait, lad, please!' he shouted.

Derruff was staring back at them, steadily and without any apparent strain, as he held the fully grown man out over the sea with just one hand. 'I will drop him,' he warned. 'If you cannot do what you promised, I will drop your friend and he will drown. He cannot swim. He's unconscious. Hold hands, friends. Do as you promised or Sam will die in the sea and I will collect what I came for and go.'

Ty yelled and tried to run at Derruff, but Bob, displaying surprising strength for a man in his seventies, yanked him to a halt and forced his face around to look at the others. 'Do as he says! Link up! NOW!' Turning to the other two, Bob slapped the Miganium, which Ty had dropped on deck in his panic, brutally between his own palm and the furious, desperate boy's. 'All of you!' shouted Bob, his face livid and his eyes glittering. 'You need to LINK! *FEEL something!* What are those men down there to you? NOTHING! Just a number! Just fifty-nine people in a newspaper headline! NOTHING! What is SAM to you?!'

Tania was crying and Darren was looking more stricken than Ty had thought possible. Derruff still held Sam over the water, his face impassive and set. The lieutenant and David Chambers were standing some way off, quite still and staring.

'Come *ON!*' yelled Bob. The four linked hands around the Miganium a second time, and as the chain was completed Ty felt a tremendous surge jolt through him. It was both hot and cold and it knocked the whole party outwards in a wave so that their heads jerked back and the circle widened, their arms taut and straining to keep a hold of each other and the Miganium.

Ty didn't know whether his eyes were open or shut, but he couldn't see the ship any more. He was in a ditch—a cold, grey muddy ditch—and there was rain on the back of his head and a boy in his arms with blood on his face. Ty suddenly realized he was inside one of Bob's worst memories. Bob, in a war zone, cradling his best friend as he died amid rubble. The young man, only twenty years old, was mouthing something, but Bob couldn't hear him. He never could hear him. The sob that shook through Ty seemed to blow the memory away and now he was in Tania's head. Tania was running, running,

running. The boy on the motorbike was shouting after her and she was terrified and hurt—a tremendous pain shot through Ty's jaw like an electric shock. Tania *hadn't* fallen off the motorbike. Her boyfriend had hit her. Ty cried out and knew that he was passing now into Darren's mind. Darren was pounding with all his strength on a bedroom window, with stickers of aeroplanes on it. It was a grey winter's day and a woman that Ty knew was Darren's mother was getting into a cab, with bags and cases. She must have been able to hear the pounding and the desperate crying of her son, who was just six years old, but she didn't look back. She never looked back at all, not even when the taxi turned at the top of the lane and disappeared from view.

Ty's own feelings and memories were scattered around. Finding Aunty Dawn waiting for him one birthday morning; his mother gone to a last minute job in the night, his dad's shirt, still hanging in the wardrobe years and years after his death; getting beaten up by Dom in front of a girl he really liked. It was an awful thing to do, thought Ty, to make them all feel these terrible feelings when they were trying so hard to help. What good could it do?

There was spray in his face and a roaring in his ears. His hands hurt badly and, as he tumbled down onto the deck with the rest of them, Ty's eyes cleared. The four of them lay in a huddle, craning their necks to look up into the sky. The most incredible geyser of water was thundering up towards the clouds, roaring like a hurricane. Derruff and Sam were now clinging together at the edge of the deck, their hair and clothes trying to tear away in the wind. Lieutenant Thompson was crouched on deck, also hanging grimly onto the railing and holding his cap, and David Chambers was next to him in an identical position.

Ty wondered just what they'd unleashed. It looked amazing and terrible, as if the sky itself was about to rip apart and unravel down to the horizon. The water channelled up to meet low clouds which had rolled in, and then arched out into an incredible fountain, which hurtled down into the churning sea and created a perfect, circular tidal wave. The wave shot out in a ripple as high as Sam's bungalow, sending the smaller craft spinning and rocking and almost capsizing them.

Ty tried to sit to see what was happening, but the spray and the wind beat him back down. It seemed to last for ever, but it was probably no more than a minute before the noise abated and the immense, furious column of water began to wobble and then flop and finally sag back to the sea, sending a last, uneven wave across the scattered flotilla around them.

The semi-submersible had weathered the chaos sturdily, with only the occasional metallic groan. As the wind died down and the last of the sea spray came to rest on the deck and all over the small, dazed party, Ty stared and stared and stared at what had been the gap of water stretching between them and the distant white painted bridge. *The American Cormorant* had raised her deck just clear of the sea. Resting there, listing slightly to one side with seawater running in torrents from its curved grey flanks, was Her Majesty's Submarine *Castleforth*.

Chapter 21

The rescue services closed in within seconds, swarming across the water and down ladders on either side of the ship to reach its crew. Special equipment was run across the metal bed of *The American Cormorant* and crews of professionals set to opening the submarine's hatch.

Ty was limp with exhaustion. They all were. Before too long his head sank back down onto the deck, aching and hot. His palms stung against the salty spray and, opening them shakily, he saw that the Miganium had burned into the skin, leaving a relief map of fine red blisters. Tania, Bob and Darren were in a similar state, slumped around him, groaning. Sam crouched down next to Ty. 'Are you OK?' he asked, anxiously. 'Yeah,' breathed Ty, faintly. 'What about you?'

'Oh—I knew he wasn't really going to chuck me in the sea,' said Sam, lightly. Ty didn't believe him. Not one of them had doubted for a second that Derruff had meant what he said. It *had* worked though, Ty had to concede. Although if he ever tried to hurt Sam again, Derruff was going to get what was coming to him, thought Ty, grimly. The very idea made his head throb again.

Bob was sitting up, looking disorientated. 'We did it,' he said, in a shell-shocked voice. The sound of helicopters overhead and more rescue and media craft tearing across the sea made it hard for any of them to talk or hear each other as Darren and Tania sat up too, wincing and painfully letting the Miganium drop onto the deck, leaving its livid blisters behind.

David Chambers seized upon a passing paramedic, who'd just been dropped from a helicopter on a winch. 'They can't fit any more on the deck down there!' they heard him shout. 'These people need seeing to!'

The paramedic stared at the odd little party on the deck and then motioned to another who was detaching himself from the same winch and waving the copter up into the air again. Both men ran across to them and, seeing they were walking wounded, began to guide them across the deck and down the hatch.

Below it was calmer and quieter. They all sat in a row along a bench beneath a white painted steel girder, feeling very odd, as the paramedics applied first cold water to their hands and then a slick of ointment, before bandaging them carefully. The medics checked in their eyes with little torches, asked them a few cursory questions, and then hastened back up on deck to get to the main action. Through his radio, David Chambers was in touch with Lieutenant Thompson. 'They're in!' he told them all excitedly. 'There are men alive in there! You did it! You did it!'

Ty smiled through his exhaustion. His heart seemed to be flapping about in his rib cage like a mad bird. Tania was openly weeping and beaming and Darren was squeezing her shoulder and shaking his head, trying not to cry too. Bob looked just as emotional and wiped his eyes carefully with his bandaged hands.

Sam sat down next to Ty and gave his hair a rough pat. 'I'm proud of you, Ty.' he said.

They didn't know what to say when Derruff climbed down through the hatch and ducked under the white girder. He had gathered all the Miganium off the deck and put it into the small steel case. 'I have to go now,' he said. 'I hope you can forgive me, Sam.'

Sam nodded. 'You did what you had to do,' he said. 'And it worked.'

'So that's it, is it?' said Tania, sniffing. 'No more powers? Nothing else?'

'Your powers will have ebbed away in twelve hours or so,' said Derruff. 'It's for the best. You've seen what you were capable of, and so did your authorities. You would have been a grave danger to your planet. If I wasn't certain that these powers would fade and die, I *would* have to kill you all.' He looked deadly serious and Darren gulped.

'But I am happy that I allowed you your last day. I am very happy that you were able to save some of your people. It's the first time I have witnessed Miganium doing good. David Chambers,' here he turned and addressed the agent, who was hovering nearby, nervously clicking his pen again. 'Do you understand everything I told you about what has happened to these people?' The agent nodded. 'Then I believe I can trust you to protect them from too much interrogation or testing.'

The man nodded again. 'We'll just need a few hours to debrief—and get our stories worked out for the press. They will be home, unharmed, by the end of tomorrow. I give you my word.'

'Good. Then I must leave,' concluded Derruff. 'There is more work to be done. You will not be troubled by Miganium again for some time.'

'For some *time?*' echoed David Chambers. 'You mean it's coming back?!'

'Oh yes,' said Derruff. 'It's travelling on a wide arc through space and I calculate that it will be back in your part of the galaxy again, and will probably pass close enough to Earth to be considered a risk. It will help if you leave notification for your successors.'

'Right . . .' said David Chambers. 'I'll do that. Should we be alerting anybody soon?'

Derruff narrowed his eyes and made a swift calculation. 'You've got 5,352 years,' he said.

Tania got to her feet and walked over to Derruff. To his surprise and confusion, she put her arms around him and kissed his cheek. 'This pushing of mouth against face?' he asked, one more time. 'What is this?'

'It's a way of saying thank you,' said Tania. 'I mean— I wasn't at all in favour of the chucking Sam in the North Sea bit, but I suppose we probably couldn't have done it without you. And well, *someone* in the universe has to say thank you.'

Derruff smiled. 'I must go now,' he said again. 'But I wish to speak with Ty alone before I do.'

Ty followed him back up on deck where they walked to the far tip of the bow; further away from emergency traffic it was slightly less noisy. Minutes later Ty was alone, with only a small piece of paper in his hand to remind him of what had happened in that incredible week. Derruff had pulled a small silvery rectangle out of his jogging top pouch and squeezed a button on it, and the low cloud that had closed in around the ship bubbled further downward and glowed with a faintly greenish light. Ty had turned and stared at it in great excitement at the prospect of seeing Derruff's spaceship.

But after a few seconds nothing happened, and when Ty turned back to look at Derruff, the alien was no longer there. The cloud flashed once and then drifted apart into wisps of ethereal mist. Nothing hovered behind it. No glowing saucer shot up into the heavens. Derruff—and the Miganium—were gone.

Inexplicably sad, Ty went back down below. Everyone looked at him with curiosity. Ty slumped back onto the bench and gulped hard.

'He just vanished,' he said. 'It's all over.'

Chapter 22

What would it be like when his brain exploded? Of course he knew that it *wouldn't*. Who ever heard of a boy's head exploding at the dentist?

But as John Payne pulled and prised and wrestled the steel off his teeth Ty did wonder about the strength of his skull. When the brace was finally off and he was doing the warm pink rinsing thing, it felt extremely odd. Although he'd never have imagined it a year ago when it was put on, Ty had got entirely used to the feel of the steel in his mouth.

John's dental nurse gave him a small hand mirror and he stared in wonder at his even, white teeth.

He went home early instead of straight back to school, wandering down the lane in the warm summer sun. Back at the house, he pushed open the front door and shouted, 'Hi! I'm back!'

'Hiya, babe!' called Aunty Dawn, from the kitchen.

Judging by the tinny screaming, *The Teddy Taylor Show* was on the little TV.

'Hello, Ty! Let me see!' Ty's mum came down the stairs and peered in fascination at his mouth, while he grinned obligingly. 'Oh! It looks brilliant!' she gasped and gave him a hug. 'My boy is growing up so handsome!'

'*Mum!*' Ty swatted her away, embarrassed but very pleased.

'Oh—I've got something for you!' said his mum. She reached into the large shoulder bag on the stair post, full of her books and notes for her teaching degree. 'The choir is going really well,' she went on, as she rummaged through her bag, 'I wish you'd join!'

'Mum, you know I can't sing like you!' laughed Ty. 'It's not my thing. Anyway, they'd take the Mickey because they all know you're my mum. And Rod fancies you.'

'Don't be silly, Ty! Here it is.' She presented him with a book on geology and meteorology, which displayed a heap of curious looking stones on its cover, some from Earth, some from space.

'It's from Dom!' she said. 'He was really keen for you to have it. Said he found it at a car boot sale and thought it was your kind of thing.'

'Brilliant!' said Ty, turning the pages.

'He's turning out to have a very good tenor voice, that Dom McGill,' murmured his mother. 'Oh and by the way—Tania called. Wanted to know if you'd be an usher at the wedding. Darren wants everyone in leopard skin jackets but she's not having any of it!'

Ty grinned. Tania had also been arguing solidly with Darren for the last few months since they got engaged, about exactly how many piercings he was allowed to wear in church. 'I'll call her back this evening,' he called. 'I've got to get to the Croft now and show off my new mouth!'

He pedalled down the street, still running the tip of his tongue over his curiously smooth teeth. He was looking forward to smiling widely at Sam and Bob. Bob had given up his council house in Manchester and moved south to be closer to Ty and Sam. He did volunteer work most days around the Croft. He and Sam were almost like father and son, sometimes, the way they argued and laughed and instinctively got on with things together. Bob was also a great help with driving the minibus when they ran courses and people needed collecting.

Ty chained his bike up near the lamppost, with some difficulty, because the numbers on the combination lock kept spinning around awkwardly. He'd been trying to ignore it for most of the day, telling himself that it wasn't going to happen. But his heart kept skittering in defiance every few minutes, clearly not in agreement.

He didn't make straight for the bungalow, but headed deeper into the woods until he found a quiet place, well away from the road or any other people. For many minutes he simply sat, listening and turning the small piece of paper over and over in his hands. On it was written *July 12*. That was all. It was a bit blurred because Derruff had scribbled it in pencil, standing on the damp deck of *The American Cormorant*.

'I've made a calculation,' he had told Ty as aircraft thundered and motorboats chugged all around them and the sea wind snatched at his words. 'I believe this is the date. Really, I should kill you.'

Ty had gazed up at him steadily, wondering whether Derruff *would* kill him. But the alien just looked back at him for a moment and then shook his head. 'In actual fact, Ty,' he said, sounding utterly unlike Teddy Taylor at that moment, 'I've never killed anyone . . . deliberately. Although I know I will if I ever have to.'

'Do you have to now?'

'No. I don't think so. Now—you won't notice anything for nearly a year. The way the Miganium works is quite mathematical and I have been able to calculate its strength, combined with your body weight and the effects of puberty. I believe this is the date. Although I may be a day out. It is possible.'

Ty shivered as Derruff handed him the small piece of paper with *July 12* written on it. 'But what about when my brace comes out?' he asked.

'It makes no difference. The Miganium has diffused into your system. Because you are so young and your cell renewal is so much faster than the others', it has embedded its traces in you for ever. You'll notice nothing for many months. It's a sort of incubation period. But you must be very careful from this date onwards.'

'Will I hurt Sam?' Ty asked, urgently.

'No. Sam will be fine.'

'So why are you letting me go? Won't I be a grave danger to the planet?'

'Possibly,' sighed Derruff. 'But I have seen something in you. You are different. You were different even before you found the Miganium. I believe you will find a good use for your powers. And I have a strange feeling that there *is* something more you are meant to do. But you know you must be careful. No tricks. No shows. Restraint. That's what you must always remember. Restraint. I can always come back, you know!' And he was grinning and chuckling when he pulled out the silvery rectangle thing and Ty turned away to stare in excitement at the sky. And, of course, that was the last Ty saw of him.

Now he stared at the piece of paper, curling in his palm. The sky overhead was clear and blue and all he could hear was the drone of insects, the chirruping of birds and the very distant thrum of a light aircraft.

Taking a deep inhalation of warm, woody air, Ty took off his watch and placed it on the ground a metre or so away. Then he held out his bare wrist and muttered, 'Come on then.'

Glinting in the late afternoon sun, the metal strap rose up on either side of the dial, undulating like a snake. With a jolt, the timepiece snagged up into the air and then flew smoothly across to Ty's wrist, flopping gently onto it, face up and curving round, ready to be fastened.

Rising, Ty did up the watch. He grinned to himself, tucked the paper in his pocket and walked off to meet Bob and Sam at the bungalow. He guessed he probably couldn't tell them. Probably.

EXCLUSIVE Q&A WITH ALI SPARKES

1. IF YOU COULD HAVE ANY SUPERPOWER, WHAT WOULD IT BE?

Shapeshifting! Definitely. I mean, being a telekinetic would be amazing too but it's the kind of thing that's hard to hide and it scares people. You'd forever be worried that you'd get arrested and chucked in a concrete bunker. Whereas if I could shift into a fox or a bird or an otter and slide away into the wild, that would be amazing. And safer than telekinesis, I think, because nobody's really scared of British wildlife! Mind you, sometimes I've stared at an object so long I've become convinced that it HAS moved and I really do have that superpower. I just haven't quite worked out how to switch it on yet . . .

2. IF *OUT OF THIS WORLD* WAS MADE INTO A BLOCKBUSTER FILM, WHICH ACTORS WOULD YOU CAST IN THE LEAD ROLES?

Ooooh—what a lovely idea! OK . . . **Tyrone** would be played by Jude Wright—the brilliant actor who plays Marcus in Simeon Goulden's fantastic *SPY* sitcom on Sky1. Although he'd have to look a bit geekier and be willing to wear a brace on his teeth.

David Tennant could play **Chambers** (English accent again, David!) and Sarah Lancashire would make a brilliant **Miss Merrill**, in a wig and orange lipstick. James McAvoy (Mr Tumnus and Professor X in *X-Men*) would do for **Sam**. Jim Broadbent for **Bob**, Jack Whitehall for **Darren**, and Jenna Louise Coleman (Doctor Who companion) would do a fine **Tania**, I think . . .

Oh and Jerry Springer would have to play **Derruff**! Or maybe David Hasselhoff . . .

3. DO YOU THINK THAT ALIEN LIFE FORMS REALLY EXIST OUT THERE?

Yes. Without a doubt. Can't believe we are the only life in this endless universe.

4. WHAT ADVICE WOULD YOU GIVE TO ANYONE WHO SUDDENLY DEVELOPS SUPERPOWERS?

Keep it quiet! And only share it with people you would trust with your life.

5. WHAT INSPIRED YOU TO WRITE *OUT OF THIS WORLD*?

I remember the US talk show thing was just getting big in the UK when I first came up with the idea. Jerry Springer, Rikki Lake, and a host of others were getting people to scream at each other and fight each other and just behave appallingly on TV for everyone's entertainment. Now we have our own UK versions. They are the worst thing on TV. And yet the hosts—even though they encourage this really hideous behaviour—seem to be treated like minor gods. It struck me then that if an alien dropped in, it might get the impression that Jerry Springer was all-powerful. So the idea of an alien assuming Jerry Springer's form was in my head and that got mixed up by a long-term obsession with telekinesis and . . . well, you know the rest.

6. Sam's survival skills really come in handy when he and Ty are hiding out in the woods. Did you have to learn any survival skills yourself when you were researching the book?

Yes. I went to Woodsmoke, which is based in Cumbria and run by some exceptional people who trained under Ray Mears (TV's Mr Survival). Ben McNutt and Lisa Fenton ran the short course I went to, where we learned how to make shelters, build fires, and gut and cook fish. It was fantastic! And, as I write this, they're still running it very successfully. Ben is thanked at the start of this and the Shapeshifter books (lots of survival stuff in those too) and Fenton Lodge in Shapeshifter is named after Lisa Fenton.

7. Why did you make Sam epileptic?

I wanted to slow the story down. I needed a good reason for Sam and Ty to take to the woods and not just jump in a car. I didn't want motorway embankments as a backdrop! So it was partly that— so that Sam couldn't drive—but also that I once interviewed an epileptic guy for a magazine article and was so affected by what he told me about the condition. I had no idea it could be so bad for the sufferer—and I was struck by how brave and resilient they have to be. I think Sam's seizures are accurately depicted and I really hope any epileptics who read it agree. It made me have a really soft spot for Sam as a character.

8. WHO IS YOUR FAVOURITE COMIC BOOK SUPERHERO AND WHY?

It used to be Batman until the films got more and more heavy and dark and miserable and then I went right off the Dark Knight. Nowadays I'd probably say Spiderman. You can't go wrong with Spiderman. (Unless you're a fly).

9. DO YOU THINK YOU'LL WRITE ANY MORE BOOKS ABOUT TY'S ADVENTURES?

I sort of already have! Ty shows up in the Shapeshifter series, as Gideon's telekinetic tutor in *Dowsing the Dead* and *Stirring the Storm*. He might also show up again in the Unleashed series . . . But another book all about Ty? Hmmm . . . well, I never say never . . . I'm very fond of him . . .

If you liked

OUT OF THIS **WORLD**

You'll love the
BRAND NEW SERIES

A group of very special teenagers. Each with an
incredible power, they live together, protected by the
government. Out in the ordinary world they know
they must not use their powers. But good intentions
are easy . . . following them through is another matter.

Turn over the page to read an extract of

UNLEASHED

Mind Over Matter

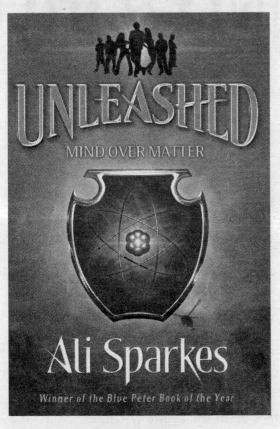

OUT NOW!

UNLEASHED

MIND OVER MATTER
OUT NOW!

A tiny avalanche of pebbles tumbled down the cliff face. They rattled musically as they bounced off large chunks of chalk, flint, and Wealden clay.

'Go on,' said Gideon, staring up at the ribbed grey curve of the Best Ammonite In The World. 'Keep going. Left and right . . . ge-e-ently . . . '

Luke nodded and held his sightline as if his pale green eyes were lasers boring into the cliff. And, in a manner of speaking, they were. The ammonite, five or six metres up in the crumbly edifice, nudged a little to the left.

'Keeeeep it coming,' said Gideon, rubbing his hands through his fluffy blond hair in tense concentration. 'As soon as it's out I'll catch it and bring it down safely . . . Yeeees . . . Just a bit further down. A biiiit furthe—*DOOF!*'

CRACK! The impact between his shoulder blades was so sudden and so forceful that the air was knocked out of his lungs and he was smacked face down into the gritty foot of the cliff. He was dimly aware that Luke had executed the same maneouvre and, as he scrambled round to see their attacker, his brother did likewise, a mirror image to his right.

Both of them were hauled up into a standing position and roughly shaken by one shoulder. Only one man held them but they knew better than to attempt to struggle out of the iron grip.

'Wh-what?' squawked Gideon, trying to sound indignant rather than guilty.

It didn't work.

'Try me!' rumbled the heavy-browed man who had them immobilized. 'Just once more.'

'U-Uncle Jem!' Gideon's eyes skittered around, trying to remind the man that the beach had people on it. *Normal* people. Admittedly, probably only about two dozen sprinkled out along the mile or so of pebbly shore, but still . . . *people.* 'We were just looking at the fossils!'

'You were *not* just looking,' growled the man, his Scottish accent deepening. Gideon had noticed that it got much more distinct when Jem was angry or stressed. 'Don't take me for an idiot, Gideon. One more trick like that and you'll be on a helicopter back to Cumbria before you can say *Oh—what happened to my holiday?*'

'What's going on in your heads?' he demanded. He took off his baseball cap, revealing close-cropped dark hair, and adjusted the almost invisible communication device inside it. 'How long have you waited for this week? Luke—you know how much it means to your mum. And yet you try to pull a Cola stunt—for what? A chunk of rock?'

Jem paused and narrowed his dark grey eyes at them. He regarded them for some time and then let his hand drop. 'It's bad enough that I have to babysit you two for a week and pretend to be your uncle,' he muttered. 'I didn't expect to have to discipline you as well.'

'You won't have to—not again!' said Gideon. 'We'll be good—perfect!'

Jem let a hint of a smile touch his mouth. 'Well—*that* wouldn't be normal and teenage would it?'

'Come on, the others are getting twitchy. Let's go and get some ice cream.' Jem turned round and headed across the beach towards a young couple who were stretched out on some beach mats. He didn't stop at their beach camp though, but just walked on along to the foot of the zigzagging cliff path, where some enterprising Islanders had set up an ice cream kiosk and a burger and hot dog stand.

Jem bought them some cones topped with a mound of fluffy white Island ice cream, each planted with a chocolate flake. They moved to a bench halfway up the cliff path to eat them, gazing back down to the beach with its sprinkling of people, brightly coloured towels, and wind breaks. Two old ladies were in fold-out chairs not far from the ice cream kiosk. The young couple they'd passed were packing up their beach mats and getting ready to go. Several bold swimmers were up to their waists in the chilly June surf. A girl with a dog was exploring one of the outcrops of pale chalky cliff face, digging at it with something and putting her finds in a battered satchel bag hanging over her shoulder. The dog—a wiry little black thing—ran up and down the slope of the crumbled cliff footings.

Her shorts and T-shirt were grubby with chalk and clay and she had some kind of ankle boots on; battered brown things with rugged soles. She did not look like a day tripper. Her limbs were lean and golden brown from regular days outdoors and she seemed entirely at ease with her task. Completely focused even when she was absent-mindedly ruffling her dog's head with one hand.

Gideon decided he fancied her. He nudged Luke and pointed down, waggling his eyebrows for effect. Luke looked and then smiled and moved his hands descriptively.

'Yup,' said Gideon. 'Definitely a bit of a babe. A rock chick. Geddit?'

Luke laughed silently.

And that was when Gideon first noticed the crack at the top of the cliff.

Three seconds later the cliff began to fall.

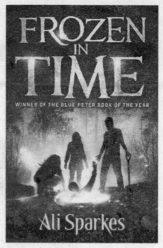

1956

Freddy and Polly are used to helping their father with his experiments. So they don't mind being put into **cryonic suspension**—having their hearts frozen until their father wakes them up again. They know it will only be for an hour or two, so there's nothing to worry about . . .

PRESENT DAY

Ben and Rachel have resigned themselves to a long, boring summer. Then they find a hidden underground vault in the garden containing two **frozen figures**, a boy and a girl. And when Rachel accidentally presses a button, something unbelievable happens . . .

*Can Polly and Freddy adapt to the twenty-first century? Will their bodies survive having been in suspension for so long? And most important of all, what happened to their father—and why did he leave them **frozen** in time?*

OUT NOW!

For more exclusive content visit

www.alisparkes.com